Every family has its secrets. But when you are suddenly the matriarch, tending the dark fires of memory, and your own mind is fading, who do you dare to share them with? Your journal or your eight-year-old granddaughter?

Interweaving diaries penned forty years apart, Kelly Simmons's captivating second novel, *The Bird House*, blends the fierce voice of Ann Biddle, a woman struggling to bond with her only grandchild, Ellie, while railing against the ravages of early dementia, with her point of view as a young wife and mother. We witness the secrets of Ann's family through every lens—from the clarity of the rearview mirror and through the haze of Alzheimer's. And we see her as a young housewife in 1960s suburbia, grappling with breast cancer, her mother's death, a disappointing marriage, a passionate affair, and a tragedy that leaves her stunned until, four decades later, her whip-smart granddaughter unwittingly sheds a burst of light on the family's shadowy history.

A subtly tense, darkly psychological tug-of-war between the present and the past, *The Bird House* is a moving treatise on family, love, and memories—both lost and found.

Also by Kelly Simmons

Standing Still

The Bird House

KELLY SIMMONS

WASHINGTON SQUARE PRESS
New York   London   Toronto   Sydney

Sim

WASHINGTON SQUARE PRESS
A Division of Simon & Schuster, Inc.
1230 Avenue of the Americas
New York, NY 10020

This Washington Square Press edition February 2011

WASHINGTON SQUARE PRESS and colophon are
trademarks of Simon & Schuster, Inc.

For information about special discounts for bulk purchases, please contact Simon
& Schuster Special Sales at 1-866-506-1949 or business@simonandschuster.com.

The Simon & Schuster Speakers Bureau can bring authors to your live event. For
more information or to book an event contact the Simon & Schuster Speakers
Bureau at 1-866-248-3049 or visit our website at www.simonspeakers.com.

Designed by Suet Yee Chong

Manufactured in the United States of America

10 9 8 7 6 5 4 3 2 1

Library of Congress Cataloging-in-Publication Data

Simmons, Kelly.
     The bird house : a novel / Kelly Simmons.
          p. cm.
     1. Family secrets—Fiction. 2. Dementia—Patients—Fiction. 3. Girls—Fiction.
4. Grandparent and child—Fiction. 5. Domestic fiction. 6. Psychological fiction.
I. Title.
 PS3619.I5598B57 2010
 813'.6—dc22
                                                              2010029298

ISBN 978-1-4391-6093-0
ISBN 978-1-4391-6405-1 (ebook)

For my grandmothers,
who knew when to keep a secret

October 22, 2010

Beneath the surface of any problem, if you scrabble a bit, you'll find a secret.

It may take a while—decades perhaps—not for your excavation, mind you, but for your *desire* to appear; for that childlike curiosity to float up again. Indeed, you may need an actual child to summon it, as I did.

But this is what drives us—the historians, the trash pickers, the gossips, the shrinks. And yes, the readers of books. We're all rooting around, teasing out other people's hidden reasons.

Haven't we all profited from another's heartache? Anything antique or inherited comes to you out of pain. And it comes to you, doesn't it? Why, even the comforting of a sniveling acquaintance carries a sweet center: after they sob on your shoulder, they will tell you *why*.

Please don't say I'm drawn to others' secrets because I have several in my own deep past. That's a bit tidy, don't you think? In fact, I'll come clean with a confession right now. Perhaps that will make you feel better about my motives.

Forty years ago, my young daughter died because of something I did. Notice I stop short of saying I killed her, even though I clearly did. No one knows this. Do you think

my daughter-in-law would ever let me near my granddaughter if she knew?

I didn't bury this pivotal event, or suffocate it in a cloud
of good works, as so many venerable Main Line ladies would,
yet much of it, the details especially, have sloughed away.
By necessity, by neglect, by a need for the widow to soldier
on. And yes, by the failure of my own memory. Call it what
you will: "senior moments," old age, dementia. It's inevitable, that's what it is. You go right ahead and complete all
the crosswords your children press on you; but know they can
keep you only so sharp.

Sometimes my memory of that awful day wanders away
completely, and when it returns, it jolts me, like falling in
dreams. I can't summon my actions in crystal detail anymore;
I see the house, that room, through a haze, in pieces. I can
see the maple tree outside the window, and beyond it, the old
field on one side and the park with the verdigris Revolution-
ary War statue on the other. But I've forgotten, for instance,
what time it was; whether the light sparkled when it hit the
water, or cast shadows across it, making it look more gray
and deeper than it actually was. I draw a blank on whether
the baby cried in the distance, or where Peter was hiding—
in the cellar; in the field; or in the small, dark shed. Parts of
it are gone, perhaps forever. I miss the details, the small in-
tricacies of many things now, even this. All the more reason
to continue to write things down in my diary. All the more
reason for me to take my pictures, to hang on to scrapbooks
and photo albums in steamer trunks. All the more reason to
collect evidence.

This morning, for instance, I completely forgot that I'd

been to the lawyer. My newest secret, and I only remembered when I opened my freezer and saw what I'd hidden there. Imagine!

It will all come out in time, the tidbits I've learned and swung round to my advantage. But I did not set out to do any of it, and neither did Ellie. It's important you believe me. The natural order of things merely took over. The drive to dig pulled us like the tides.

All we did, after all, was pay attention. You should try it sometime. Watch a woman's face as she fingers her antique locket. Hear the jangle of charm bracelets covering up an ancestor's cries. Feel the ring handed down from grandmother to mother to daughter, how the gold is worn down at the back by everything they'd done while wearing it—all the games they'd played, all the people they'd touched, all the things they'd held and broken.

It's all there, in every jewelry box and trunk, every photo album and yellowed postcard, every attic and basement. Just look, and you'll see what I mean. You don't have to travel to a lost city to find the artifacts of a mysterious society. Just go ask your grandmother.

July 1, 2010

THREE MONTHS EARLIER

Earlier this week, I positioned navy and red cushions on the porch chairs, tucked blue pansies into planters, and hung an enormous flag. It flaps so loudly on breezy nights I think a man in a canvas raincoat has entered the room. It was one of those days when I missed Theo dearly. After all, it takes one to hold the ladder and one to climb it.

I don't normally approve of such obvious seasonal decor, but Ellie was coming over and I wanted her parents—my son, Tom, and his wife, Tinsley—to know that I was quite aware, fully cognizant, of the upcoming holiday.

Of course I can't remember every single thing; who can? Maybe that's why I took up photography so late in life, started lugging Theo's Nikon camera around. So I could document things, remember them, the way he used to. The stages of the buildings he designed were as fleeting as memory, after all; once the plaster covered the fragile wooden bones you never saw them again. Even when they were finished, completed, they changed by the season. Everything changes, even the way we look at it. I remember Theo used to lay out the progression of construction photos across his big desk, and explain each step to me, and what had gone right and what had gone wrong. In the beginning, before we had children, I sat on the corner of that desk with my chin on his shoulder and listened as he explained the engineering dilemmas and described the imported materials. He taught me about divided light and molding, about soffits and cupolas, giving names to things I'd seen but never truly known.

On the weekends, after we made the rounds of the tag sales, Theo and I would sneak into Realtors' open houses, pretending to be in the market, and Theo would whisper in my ear the flaws and strengths of each floor plan. The den was too dark, the bedrooms too small. The kitchen should be reoriented to face south. These were our jigsaw puzzles; this was our cinema. When the children arrived, it was as if there was no room for our home life in his work life. I heard their voices, not his. And he heard his clients, no one else. That's what I remember, and of course Theo isn't here to refute me. There's a certain glory in that, I tell you. Widowhood means I'll always have the last damn word.

I invited Ellie over for more than just the Fourth of July. I forgot some of what the lawyer told me to do—but no matter. I believe I managed to collect what he needed. I do remember him saying it should be simple, and he was right—it was easy to execute, childlike, almost, except for one part.

Ellie arrived to spend the night and I didn't even have to ask if she was thirsty. Aren't all eight-year-old girls thirsty? I simply set out a glass of Coca-Cola next to the tray of sparklers and that little blond head bobbed straight for it, moth to flame. Why, I could have poisoned her, easily, with that amber glass.

When she finished drinking I brought out the fireworks

jigsaw puzzle, then made a big show of needing to do the dishes, so Ellie didn't think twice about me ferrying away her tumbler while wearing rubber gloves. I sealed it in a plastic bag and put it the freezer, just as George Marquardt Esquire told me to. Well, he told me to put *something* in the freezer.

The whole business reminded me briefly of a game I used to play with my father. Whenever he returned from one of what my mother called "his adventures"—a safari, a trek of some kind, a bird-watching expedition—he'd bring me back a present and hide it somewhere symbolic in the house, while providing only the barest of clues. This was no small undertaking, searching for these treasures, as we had ten bedrooms, eight baths, and, as I recall, many similar rooms with different names: den, office, library, sitting room. They had minor differences among them—the library had books and the den had taxidermy—but only the bedrooms seemed wholly differentiated, as each was a different pale color. Salmon, gold, mint. I console myself with the lack of memory by reminding myself that *ten* is quite a few of anything for anyone to recall. At any rate, I do distinctly remember my father hiding an Inuit doll in our freezer, of all places. (It was wildly unfair, the freezer being totally out of reach for a young girl, yet completely appropriate as a stand-in for tundra.) As I closed my own freezer door I heard the solid, reassuring hum that signaled its frosty seal, and I wondered about that doll. I'd thrown out most of my father's gifts, and given some to my mother to sell at auction. But I couldn't picture the doll. Pity; perhaps Ellie would have liked it.

Later that night, we watched the fireworks from the deck off my bedroom. They were far enough away that we could appreciate their expanse, but close enough that they were terribly loud, and Ellie snuggled into the curve of my shoulder during several startling booms. Afterward I taught her how to light and hold a sparkler, and she promptly went through the whole box, her blond curls bouncing as she wrote her name and mine in the sky. When I close my eyes I can still see them there, the loops of her *e*'s and the bumps of my *n*'s burning an electric trail.

Theo and I had done that with sparklers, too, on one of our earliest dates. He took me for a walk in the evening near the library, around the art museum circle. We sat on the towering steps in the dark and when he reached into his book bag and pulled out the sparklers I was struck by the romance of it, by his organization and forward thinking. Not by his thriftiness, or the student-y simplicity of the date. Funny the things you remember and the things you forget. He always had sparklers for Tom, too, and now I had them for Ellie.

It had grown late, and a mere ten minutes after the last sparkler fizzled down to a glowing silver nub, Ellie fell asleep clutching her worn stuffed bear and breathing heavily, mouth open, in the guest room. I call it the guest room, but it used to have another name, another purpose. Another child once slept in it, in another life, in another bed. I didn't remove anything; only Theo, of course, would have thought to change the furniture. He was the one who spent a whole weekend putting away her toys and books and clothes, keeping only a few cherished photographs around. One day I walked in and her maple canopy bed was gone; a wrought-iron headboard as delicate as filigree jewelry stood in its place. It was impossible to imagine my daughter against that frilly backdrop, and

I suppose that's why he chose it. Its pattern circled round and round; you could lose yourself trying to find your way out of its curves and whorls.

I stood over Ellie a long time, making certain she was fast asleep before I stepped forward and snipped a locket of her golden hair. It was only when I stood above her with my sharpest scissors that I realized the import of what I was doing. The scene below me—the cottony pillow interrupted by the swirl of flaxen hair; the graceful indents below her ears; her neck, as tiny as an animal's, pulsing with her soft breath—was something only a mother or a criminal would be privileged to see. Or someone, like me, who was both.

February 11, 2010

Yes, I've taken up my journal again after many years away. Let's see how long I can sustain it. I gave it up twice before; once, when my father left, and then a second time after all that business with Peter and my daughter. It's as if I knew there were some things I wouldn't need to write down to render them indelible. I remember, for instance, that both of these men cried the exact same way, their tears so heavy they made an audible splash. My father's rained on the letter he held out to me. Peter's plunked on the wax paper of the cheeseburger he'd brought from that greasy spoon we used to go to. Parting gifts. After everything else fades, we seem to remember what people give us last, don't we?

It hardly seems fair, since we get the best of everyone at the beginning. My father, in particular, seemed to float through the rooms of my youth, carried in on a cloud, all smiles and ease. My mother's cheeks always flushed in welcome; it was like witnessing roses at the precise moment they unfurled. But when my father left us, her cheeks went pale, and stayed pale. She never looked healthy again. When I stare in my own mirror, I'm always happy to see a sprinkle of brown sunspots, a constellation of blue veins, or a red-rimmed eye. At least there is color. Where there is color, there is life.

I've started writing because two interesting things have happened. I find them ironic as well, although in the fifties, "ironic" was a term we Bryn Mawr English majors could stay up all night debating the nuances of, the way my daughter-in-law goes on and on about cacao percentages in chocolate, or how much artificial sweetener or sodium is in every box on my pantry shelf. (If you've ever wondered what a housewife "does all day," well, these days I'd say they scrutinize nutritional content.)

One: I have begun to grow close to a child who is a girl, when I thought I never could again. Two: I have taken to bathing after more than thirty-five years of showering. A seventy-year-old dog, back to ancient tricks.

The girl is my granddaughter, Ellie. Tom's daughter, although to be fair, there is much of her mother about her. Organized and something of a perfectionist, just like my daughter-in-law, Tinsley, who graduated first in her class and runs a gift business out of her attic and still manages to keep her house spotless and exercise every day. Tinsley has always seemed so much happier and more organized at home than I ever was with my children. Always baking cookies and blowing bubbles and painting faces with these crayons that wash right off. But then, she has only one: Ellie.

Everything I found difficult about Ellie at three years of age (a stage I have always disliked) has fallen off her now at eight, revealing a pink new self. I guess, given my lack of involvement, and the fact that her father works so hard, that this is mainly her mother's doing. She has raised her well.

Even her name suits her. She is not an Ellen or an Eleanor. Tinsley could have named her something snappier, and last-name-ish, more like her own name. I know they toyed with naming her after Tom's sister, but didn't, to my eternal relief. Tinsley's aunt suggested Ellie be named Lucretia, after her grandmother, then called Lulu. Lucretia, a name for a corpse. Lulu, a name for a dog. This old Philadelphia business of naming everyone after someone else, then giving them a fresh, sporty nickname—ridiculous!

Tom and Tinsley might have added to Ellie, chosen Shelley or Nellie, embellished a bit, but they knew, perhaps, that she would end up pared down, straightforward and true. Tom was guileless as a child, trusting and open, easily hurt. Not Ellie.

She speaks her mind without whining. She looks you in the eye, she shakes hands. Not a firecracker, as some amusing children are, but an *arrow*.

I confess to a soupçon of relief that she isn't a gentle soul like Tom. Those openhearted qualities are so much more delectable in boys than girls. Even as a toddler, Tom was always doing sweet things. I remember he charmed Betsy and the other mothers in the neighborhood when he helped me plant flowers, and dutifully watered them every morning. I have a picture somewhere of him—one of the first decent ones I ever took with Theo's camera—struggling to carry a brass watering can that was nearly as large as he was. A darling photograph, but only because he was a boy. Let's face it: a softhearted girl eventually becomes a cliché. But Ellie? Ellie isn't like that.

That's what started drawing me to her after years at

arm's length. I confess to it all, these past years—to half cuddling and faux cooing; to giving envelopes when there should have been gifts. I did only the minimum. At Harriton Tennis Club the post-round-robin lunches throbbed with the ladies' swollen conceits of whose grandchild won what, played what, sang what. Oh, the tales of toe shoes and tumbling, of minuets, coxswains, and dressage! I sat through them mutely, with nothing to offer. I'd seen her at her birth, her christening, all the major holidays. But I didn't know, then, if she preferred dogs or cats. I didn't know her favorite color was purple. I didn't know if she could sing or whistle or turn a cartwheel. In the last six months, I've seen her perform *all three*. Betsy, my neighbor and doubles partner, says it took me a while to warm up to my only grandchild, but that's clearly not the case. In the past year, it was Ellie who shape-shifted. She came closer to me, not the other way round.

For my birthday a few months ago she baked me a cake *herself*. When I asked what was in it, she said it was a "secret family recipe." The cheek! And the last time I had dinner at Tom and Tinsley's, a few weeks ago, she presented me with a painting she called a "self-portrait." It was all bright colors, sprays of yellow hair, slashes of green eyes and red lips, and had a bit of Picasso about it—a kind of knowing crookedness. I was grateful to Tinsley for sharing something so precious. I can't tell you how many years it has been since I had a child's drawing on my refrigerator. When I anchored it there, magnets on all four sides to keep it from curling, something enormous rose in my chest. Swells of pride in the deep waters of grief. Looking at it yesterday, I almost knew something big was going to happen; knew she had something to tell me, and then she did. Called me herself.

I took a longer bath than usual today because of the light in the room: speckled, almost fractured as it spilled from east to west. Made me wish my camera was nearby instead of hanging on the hook in the entryway. New tubs are deeper and longer—soaking tubs, they call them, which strikes me as redundant—but they feel like swimming pools to someone my size. In my old tub, I can stretch my legs all the way out, and rest my neck back over the curved lip, just so. It fits me. It's mine. And if the words "claw-footed tub" evoke something visceral, scrabbling and dark, well, fine. I take that, too, the bitter with the sweet.

Since Theo died I've had no desire to redo the bathroom or kitchen, to rearrange the furniture, let alone move. Over the years I've grown quite accustomed to the pieces Theo and I discovered at all those estate auctions in Gladwyne or Greenville—though I confess he always favored the beautiful over the comfortable. Wasn't that why he chose me? In the early days, we'd go to an auction nearly every weekend, and I'd tease him by stretching or scratching my nose when bidding began on expensive pieces. He'd swat me with his bidding number and I'd tickle him in retaliation. We'd strap our finds to the roof of Theo's old Saab and when we got them home, polish them with oil or wax, and try them in different rooms. Nothing made Theo happier than rearranging furniture.

Now I scan our possessions with their lack of upholstery and curve, and think he was just preparing me for old age—

get used to the hard backed, the flat bottomed, the squeeze in, the sit up straight. Life is a ladder-back chair. I still remember how stiffly he sat, how damned *upright* he could be. Was it to compensate for a job that required him to bend downward, poring over his blueprints, his notes and plans? Theo was barely five ten, but he looked taller, with his graceful neck and arms. Even the cowlicks in the front of his hair brought the eye upward. In one corner of the bathroom I have the chair from the den: a plain Shaker style with a navy toile cushion. Some days when I look at it I see Theo smiling ever so slightly as he carried it over his head to the car, the tag still on it; some days I see him perched on it, designing a building he loved; and some days I see his legs crumpled under him on the tennis court, spindly and thin, a paler version of the legs of his chair.

As I soak in the water, I wonder what piece of our furniture would have reminded Theo of me. And that, of course, is precisely the kind of question I might have asked him in the dark twilight as I lay in his arms; and exactly the kind of question he would have been clinically unable to answer. He was a doer, not a talker.

There is one blessing in Theo's antiques. The older I get, the more I take comfort in being surrounded by something more ancient. At last, younger by comparison!

Of course many of my old things aren't quite quaint any-more. Like the fat black answering machine that's separate from the phone and insists on squawking when I take my bath. I hear all manner of nonsense: receptionists confirming doctor appointments as if it were tea with the queen, Robert

Redford calling to remind me to save the earth, Betsy asking if I forgot about the tennis clinic (which I did). I listen and don't move. The early sun hits the windowpanes and scatters, spinning cracked rainbow circles whenever I move in the water. It's the sort of thing that would fascinate a baby or a cat. By spring the light in the bathroom and bedroom will be hazy, filtered, a green-yellow instead of its current yellow-white. Or is that summer? I can't recall. Part of me wishes I'd kept a photo journal instead of a diary, just to chronicle the light properly. I remember once, on a particularly bright winter morning, as I lay warm and enveloped in our bed, I asked Theo to join me. Well, "ask" isn't truly the proper word; I dangled my arm outside the tangle of covers and grasped his fingers as he walked by. He was heading to the bathroom to brush his teeth. His starched shirt made crisp noises as he walked. He wore brown-and-blue suspenders and he'd tucked his tie in his shirt to save it from his three-minute egg. I said nothing, just smiled and lifted one eyebrow. And he looked at me oddly, the way he did more and more in those days, as if I'd spoken too quickly, overlapping my words and rendering them foreign. He said he had to go to work, and I dropped his fingers and he went in and brushed his teeth. The sound of the bristles against his gums, doing their ugly work, was like an assault, as if he was scrubbing me away. I wonder if I'd find that moment catalogued in my old diary. I wonder if I'd find others that hurt me more.

Some find it silly, the old habit of writing things down. Betsy calls it "Victorian therapy." Here on the Main Line, we live among people who don't think too much about their lives. I'm just as guilty—writing it down is not the same as contemplating it, I assure you. However, it provides some assurance that one will *remember* it.

The last call before Ellie's was a message from Jaxie, the hostess of our book group. She calls me every month now, to remind me, and to tell me to please bring salad. Salad, as if that was simple, with the produce selections, the washing, the chopping, the pressure of a homemade dressing. In the time salad takes, a pie could be cooling on the sill. As always, I feel no urge to get up and answer the phone, dripping in a towel, to talk to anyone or write anything down. No wonder I'm forgetful!

But then Ellie's voice comes on, and I'm half tempted to pop out soaking wet and pick up the phone. Instead, I stay, and I smile. She has a husky sound to her, earthy, like Tinsley's voice. Tinsley has always sounded lovely and charming on the phone. She and Tom had met that way, on the phone, when she solicited him to join an organization at college. He'd fallen in love, he'd once confessed to me, before he'd even laid eyes on her tawny hair and hazel eyes.

"Grandma," Ellie says breathlessly, "I need you for an important homework project. It's called 'Generations' and it's an oral history of our family. So call me back right away and let me know when we can get started, okay? We've got a lot of work to do, and my mom says we have to work out a time line, so call me back, okay, bye!"

Oral history? That sounded a bit like medicine, sour and unswallowable. The things these teachers think of! Nothing an assignment, everything a *project*. As if children were archeologists or journalists. As if family truths weren't better off untold. Who fell out of love with whom. Who lost whose money. Who ran off to God-knows-where. Who never spoke to whom again. I don't think Tom was ever assigned such a thing; I'll have to ask him.

This would be tricky, I thought. But what she probably wants is a family tree or photographs. Lord knows I have plenty of photos of myself and Theo to give Ellie, if that's all she wants. Theo when he was handsome and young and driven, back in the days when we admired ambition, and didn't see it as heart disease waiting to happen. I remember the photo from the night of my engagement party, at Aunt Caro's house. Taken at twilight, the fireflies flashing green at the edges of the frame. After all the hoopla and toasts, Theo took me out on the back porch, the heady scent of spring lilacs still in the night air, and told me we'd have beautiful gardens one day, too.

"Yes, we will," I said, smiling, "because I'm going to plant them."

"Oh, no," he mock-protested, knowing what was coming.

"Yes, our humble home will teem with roses before you know it," I teased and he put his arm around me and kissed my hair. Theo thought roses were overused and overbred, and he preferred less formal flowers, things that drooped and swayed in the breeze.

"I tell you what," he said, "I'll plan and plant the flower beds if you water and weed them."

"Deal," I said, and we walked back in, arm in arm, as if it was really going to be that easy.

I soap up my arms and legs, then duck underneath the water to rinse. In addition to photos, I have stubs from the

theater, business clippings from the *Inquirer,* obituaries written and awards given, the natural ephemera of a long life.
Ellie will likely be equipped with her own flotsam of course:
markers, colored pencils, construction paper, poster board in
every color. Tinsley has kitted out her bedroom like an el-
ementary school cloakroom with its pegs and cubbyholes and
art supplies. How long will that last? How long can she enjoy
sharpening her pencils every night, running her fingers across
them, comforted by their presence, like lead soldiers standing
sentry in their case? How much time before socks and bras
are scattered, candy wrappers everywhere? That's my deepest
fear when I shut my eyes in the bathtub: Ellie's future. The
horrible half women all girls become. She'll reject her mother
and father. She'll reject me eventually, too.

I shudder. The bath has cooled. A slight breeze leaks
from the lowest corner of the window where the ivory lace
curtain doesn't quite brush the ledge. It's shrunk over the
years, as I have, and now it's shorter on the left than the right,
something that would have bothered Theo, but not me. He
was always straightening pictures, moving a vase or a candle
one inch to the left or the right, as if he was setting a stage or
taking a picture. He'd cock his head, then squint to focus in
on something, then decide, like God, where it needed to be.

I sigh as I stand, the breath bringing me up. Some of the
water drips off my left breast like a ski slope; the rest of it
finds a faster path, running straight down the empty right
side of my chest. I should be thankful, I know, that one breast
remains. That I have exactly half what I used to.

Some days I am. It is easier to find that grace in the tub
than the shower. The pounding rivulets on the right side used

to vibrate and thrum like hard rain on a flat roof. I am well rid of my shower.

Yes, some days I am thankful just for being upright. Grateful I can get in and out of things without fanfare or contraption. That I can walk up stairs and play tennis. My knees are fine and so is my back, and most days my memory is steady enough. I am here, Ellie. I need no pink ribbon to trumpet my ordinary survival. I am not to be wept over or admired or donated to. I am not quite whole, but I am here. I was spared. I'm here to tell the future about the past.

Together, we will construct some kind of history. Not the real history, of course—I'll spare your classmates the tales of death and disease and embezzlement, of women who got in over their heads. I won't tell them how my mother took all her meals at friends' country clubs when she ran out of money, or how I refused to let my own father walk me down the aisle. There is no need to scare you, Ellie. We'll build one that's more romantic and colorful, one that will glean an A. I'll make Theo's architecture career more illustrious, perhaps. I'll credit him with rebuilding the Philadelphia waterfront, instead of the strip malls dotting the turnpike. I'll say he was a man devoted to his family, instead of a man who was devoted only to his work. I'll emphasize my own feminist protests, my radical leanings. I'll speak of the time mothers circled bulldozers about to demolish Haverford Park. How we collected for UNICEF and dialed back our thermostats and rode bicycles to Bryn Mawr Market to save gas for Jimmy Carter.

I won't discuss my efforts to make Theo or myself a better person. The projects and hobbies taken up like molds I could press us into. The surprise when we walked away from

the ballroom dance studio or potter's wheel unchanged. No.
I won't speak of how he closed himself off from me after we
lost our daughter, how he used his drafting pencils to draw
a taut boundary around himself, a room with no window or
door. It was years before I realized it wasn't grief; on some
level, he had been that way all along: he had his work, and I
had him, and that was supposed to be enough. But it isn't, is
it? It never is.

Of course there are many things that will be safe to tell
you, Ellie. Good to say, even. There are a few I remember
entirely, that shine crystalline and whole in my memory. Like
that summer after Tom was born, how the fireworks were
set off at intervals up and down the Main Line. You could
look left or right and see sparks and sprays for hours. Everyone stood on their roofs and decks, and all you could hear
between the pops and streaks were sighs and exclamations.
Nothing but beauty and the contemplation of beauty. No
matter what horrible things had happened to any of us, for
one evening, there was nothing else.

I don't consider, not for one second, doing the practical,
truly safe thing—asking if Grandma Blankenship couldn't
help instead. No, I'm selfish. I want Ellie to sit with me and
go over the project, not her other grandmother. I want her to
ask *me* her questions. I want to help frame the assignment, to
draw conclusions and look for symbolism and personification
and theme. I may not have used my English major to work,
but after all these years of journal keeping, I've learned what
to show and what to hide.

And oh, the thought of her understanding! The nod, the
small smile, the light in her eyes!

I want it all now, I want too much. I want to show her off at the old Gladwyne lunch counter and answer her questions between bites of tuna salad. I want to see her slightly furrowed brow as she bends toward her notebook and ignores her homemade potato chips. Afterward I want her to sit at my antique desk. I want my high arched ceilings to echo the glide of her pencil on paper, the soft puff that emanates from her lips as she blows the pink dust of the eraser into the air. It will linger there for a moment, a writer's jet stream, before it joins the mites and pollen of my house, microscopic evidence of what we've done wrong and made right again.

I dried off quickly and called her back while I was still in my robe.

"Sorry I missed your call, Ellie," I said. "I was in the bath."

"Does your tub have those safety grips in it?"

"No," I laugh. You don't lie to a child like Ellie.

"'Cause Courtney's grandmother broke her hip when she slipped in the tub. They have all kinds of them at the hardware store, like flowers and circles."

"Really?"

"They have glue on one side and are kind of sandpapery on the other."

"Well, I'll have to look into that, then. Thank you for the information."

How can you not love a person who worries just a little, just the right amount, over you?

I suppose we've all known people who could never find the right balance between neglectful and fawning. But oh, when someone does. How often did that happen in a lifetime? Twice?

"Okay, so we need to figure out when we can work on my Generations project together."

"Indeed. How much time do you think we'll need? An afternoon?"

"Oh, more than that, Grandma. It has to be ten to fifteen pages!"

"Well, then," I exclaimed, "we might need to hire some assistants! When is it due?"

"In three weeks."

"Why don't we start with twice a week, after school? You and your mother figure out which days are best and let me know. In the meantime, I'll sharpen my pencils."

"No, Grandma, sharpen your memory! I need you to tell me stuff about the family."

"I'll do my best."

It struck me after that phone conversation that Ellie's clearness and grace reminded me of Peter Littleton. Not the Peter of now, sunburned and bloated, but the Peter of long ago, the Peter who was my lover, and before that, my high school sweetheart. What a waste, to be chaste in high school. What silly fools we were. Were we saving ourselves for infidelity, for cheating and lies?

I think of how we slow-danced at the sock hops, how we held each other too close. When the song ended, our cheeks were flushed and damp, and they made the smallest sound as we pulled apart. I still remember it; it's mixed in with the rustle of taffeta and the scuff of white bucks across an old oak floor. And later, much later, after we'd broken up because our colleges were too far apart, after he ran into me at Christmas break one year with Leo Comstock, and the next year with Theo, after both of us had married and lost track of each other—then, only then, were there other sounds, bouncy and breathy and bright. Theo was always so quiet; he arrived in the bedroom in stocking feet, his oxfords in shoe trees in the hall closet. He always undressed carefully, hanging his trousers on the valet by the bed. Placing his nickels and pennies in the leather tray on the dresser, never tossing them. But Peter! Oh! That night at our reunion held not the music of the band, but the music of his silver belt buckle, the pop of the first button, the glide of our zippers . . . and the surprising warmth of what lay inside. Like a perfectly prepared picnic basket, full of things someone else has packed, but you know you are going to lay out on the ground and love.

Where is that person now? I wonder. When I glimpse Peter occasionally at the post office, or the farmers' market, it's always in passing. He doesn't see me. Perhaps I am as unrecognizable to him as he is to me. It's always a bit of a shock—not that he could grow lumpy and pink, but that I must have been prescient; I saw it coming. Perhaps I got out just in time.

Betsy tells me that among her divorced or widowed friends who are dating, it's common practice to exchange photos of themselves in their youth. They display them on the mantel or the piano, and we both find this amusing. *Look! My barnacle was once a shiny conch shell!* And though it's also vaguely disturbing, like having a photo of a stranger on your fireplace mantel, Peter's transformation makes me understand it better. Whoever Peter dates when his wife dies would be proud to have a photo of him at twenty-eight or eighteen. Not because he was so exceptional looking, but because he *shone*. With eagerness, with curiosity, with metallic rhythm. He leaned toward the world, as if he knew there was a good story about to be told.

But I see now, in his eyes, when I glimpse him two or three times a year, that he believes his wife will live forever. Part of me wants to reach out to him again, to try to say the right thing to him as he once did to me. To tell him that nothing is forever unless you choose it to be.

Things change. People come and go. If a little girl can delight me once again, Peter, isn't anything possible?

May 4, 1967

sitz bath
orange juice

I GOT IN THE BATHTUB quickly, before the children woke up again. The heat soothed my bottom; it was still a bit sore even after four months. Dr. Kellogg said this happened more frequently in older mothers, which irritated me. Even my mother, who considered unmarried women of twenty-two spinsters, wouldn't have put me out to pasture at thirty. But some days I do feel as old as a gray washcloth. Flat and dry and stiff. The bath swells me up, plumps me like a grape, and I regain a little buoyancy. But how many times a day can a person take a bath?

No one tells you about that part of childbirth, the pain afterward. After my first baby, I asked Theo to go buy me one of those red rubber doughnuts that make it easier to sit, and you would have thought I'd asked him to lance a wound. He was not good with injury. He was not good with change. He liked order, and I suppose he'd imagined a life with children being akin to running a school. Right now it's a far sight closer to running a hospital. I imagine the idea of a piece of medical equipment in his home offended his sense of interior design.

"Do you have to have it today?" he finally said.

"I would prefer to have had it yesterday," I replied.

He looked at his watch and telegraphed a whole story with that one small movement. A story he didn't need to tell me again. He had a meeting, and couldn't figure out when he could get to the store. He could build a skyscraper, but he couldn't engineer a simple errand.

When I asked my mother about how she managed the swelling and pain, she, always decorous, claimed she didn't recall. She had a faraway look in her eyes when I asked, as if she was searching the atmosphere for an answer, and not her memory. I couldn't help thinking: I bet my father would remember. Not because he was more sensitive, but because he was more aware. When I was a child he seemed to know I was going to cry before I did. Once, when I tripped leaving our gazebo and fell against the rocks circling the hydrangeas, one of his hands reached for me, and the other, I swear, went into his pocket for his handkerchief. The hankie arrived, gently daubing at the corner of my eye, at the precise moment the first tear fell. Years later, he waited for more tears, ready to dry them, to hold me, but I wouldn't give him the satisfaction.

Of course, it's not my mother's fault that bad memories elude her. I don't blame her for blanking out the pain; for wanting to remember only the good things, the early things. She can't remember what the nursing home staff brought her for breakfast most days, but she remembers Christmas in Vienna with Aunt Caro and Aunt Lillian, and riding in a horse-drawn carriage with a Santa who couldn't speak English. She kept trying to tell him what she wanted for Christmas, and he nodded over and over again until she started to think he was mechanized. She's told me this story five or six times, and I find myself nodding the same way. The Viennese nod—useful in so many situations. She can't remember where she put her reading glasses, but she remembers the first time she went to the Louvre wearing a miniature black beret. She can't remember why my father left her, but she remembers she was wearing a red dress and red lipstick when she met him.

Even if she could remember, how bad could postpartum be when you had a personal maid and a nanny in your household, people who slept down the hall? I'm sure Bertha and Louise brought her hot compresses, poached eggs, chamomile tea. I've taken to writing down what I have for breakfast and when I bathe, to try to keep track of those elusive necessities. My neighbor Betsy says that should be my only goal for the day: to have a bath and eat breakfast. That way, she theorized, you won't be as annoyed when the rest of the day unravels, when the children and their needs take over. I wish Theo and I could have a nanny like dear old Louise. She fed me and changed me, no doubt, while my mother slept in her Lanz nightgown. Soundly, the way Theo sleeps. Neither of them prepared for this life of constantly waking up. But was I? Who was, when you're descended from people who had staff to care for the children and clean the house? The money for such things doesn't exist in our families anymore, but does the taste for them, the craving in the dark recesses of your DNA, ever go away?

Theo left the house early, before seven, complaining he couldn't sleep. You're not supposed to sleep, I told him.

"Babies' cries," I yawned, "are designed to wake up their parents. To ensure the continuation of the species."

"Is it my imagination," he sighed, "or does he cry more than I remember?"

"It's just a different timbre from Emma's," I said, pulling the pillow over my head. I could still hear the baby through the heavy layers of goose down. In some ways, muffled cries sound worse, the music of being smothered.

I couldn't see Theo's eyes, those bright eyes that had been my undoing, but I could feel them on me, the way I often did when I used an unusual word. "Timbre." Staring at me, as if he was turning me into whatever I'd said. My wife is an exotic curiosity. I must stare at her and decide if she is real or not. When I was in my last year at Bryn Mawr, we'd all take the train into Philadelphia to do research at the Free Library. The college library was too claustrophobic, too familiar; the books we needed had always been taken and the people we least wanted to see were always there. The Free Library was just the opposite; it was enormous, drafty, overwhelming. It had, if anything, too much possibility. It was filled with students, too, of course, but rarely the same cast of characters. Except for Theo, who escaped the Penn library every Thursday and Friday. My friends used to tease me: that man with eyes the color of his blueprints is staring at you again. We all thought he was soulful and deep, because his eyes were. It's a mistake to judge someone by a physical characteristic, I know now, like ascribing human qualities to pets. It's not the mark of someone soulful and deep to wait a month before you speak to a woman you desire; it's the mark of someone who has nothing to say. The mark of someone who has allowed his eyes to do the talking his entire life.

"If the crying disturbs you," I said, the disgust in my voice filtered a bit by the pillow, "you could consider rocking him."

I had been the one up nursing the baby through his ear-splitting demands, gritting my teeth through the pain of what had to be another clogged milk duct, on the right side this time. I was the one soothing him in Aunt Caro's rocking chair, not Theo. I got up, and he snored away. I'd love to know when he felt his sleep was interrupted.

"I'll get my own breakfast," he said, kissing the top of my head. Our bed was so small—one of those turn-of-the-century hand-carved frames too impractical to use, but too beautiful to part with—that he didn't have to reach far to do it. When one of us tossed and turned in the night, we often rolled into each other. This was once just an excuse for love-making; lately it made me feel jolted, bruised. I was aware of all the angles of his body, jutting elbows, knees. When his cold feet sought mine instinctively in the night, his ankle bones seemed to slice my skin.

"And . . . I'll buy lunch out today." He waited after he said it, hoping for me to thank him, I suppose, but I didn't, and he left. Betsy once said I'd created a monster by making him lunch in the first place. By tending to Theo like a garden that would blossom and eventually give me joy. Betsy always told her version of the truth, and I tried to tell her mine. I tried to tell her how much money we saved on those lunches. How the lunch box itself gave me pleasure, the tidiness of it, the napkin wrapped around the fork, the carton of milk, the silver rocket ships of leftover stew or coq au vin, the foil-wrapped present of pie. Beautiful and pulled together, like Theo was. I believed his beauty could make up for all the shortcomings, like a house with great street presence. But houses need to give you comfort. Houses need to keep you company. You live on the inside of a house, not the outside.

It was impossible to explain a beautiful lunch box, a watered window box, or an organized linen closet to a woman like Betsy, who threw her bras and panties and socks into her drawers without folding them. You know, Ann, she'd say, watching me slice Theo's meat-loaf sandwich into triangles, Theo's not your son. And it stung. Stung for years. No matter how close Betsy and I become, there is always a small crevice between us, a crevice that contains that sentence.

Of course, I have my son now, and I see the difference. He is not Theo, and Theo is not him. He doesn't even recognize his cries. Can't imagine that desperate high-pitched wail as his own.

I stayed in the bath until the last possible moment. Outside the door, the baby fussed in his crib and Emma whined in the hallway, and still I stayed in, letting the water soothe my bottom and my sore right breast. For just a few seconds more, I stayed.

February 16, 2010

Ellie is coming over tomorrow after her violin lesson, which is a few blocks away, and staying for an early supper. On the phone she asked, tentatively, what I would be serving, as if she knew it was bad manners to ask, then turned and whispered "macaroni and cheese" to her mother, who was clearly standing nearby, requesting an answer. I hadn't seen her in a few months but I imagined she still liked cheese. At the last minute, I added, "Tell her it will be homemade. With organic cheddar cheese. From Whole Foods." Oh, I was really laying it on, wasn't I? I was also lying, as I'd never even set foot in Whole Foods, which is on Tinsley's end of town, not mine.

But what did Tinsley think? That my cupboards are bare? That I've forgotten what little girls eat? I'd always thought of her as highly organized but I was beginning to suspect she was a control freak. Tom told me once it was because she skipped a grade in school, and had gone to college a year younger than everyone else. Said she was always trying to catch up, trying to prove herself to be grown up and mature and "together." She's been an adult her whole life, Mother, he'd said. Well, she didn't need to tell this particular adult what to feed a child!

I still remember my own tea parties, the pale cups, mar-
zipan apples, and soft sandwiches my mother helped Bertha
assemble in the butler's pantry near the patio. I remember her
laughing and telling Bertha it didn't matter what you put in a
tea party sandwich as long as it wasn't green and you cut the
crusts off. She was right; my mother couldn't boil an egg, but
with children it was all about color and presentation. That
was something Theo had never really understood. He winced
when I'd bring home a plastic truck or a bright clown; he'd
rub his head Christmas morning as if the shiny toys and metallic paper hurt his eyes. He liked wood, brass, leather. Toy
trains were fine but matchbox cars were frowned upon. Toy
soldiers were acceptable but those wind-up tin monkeys had
to go. The pale blue walls in Tom's room were a compromise;
Theo couldn't stand the idea of childish wallpaper. The walls
are still blue, but it's not a bedroom anymore. There is no crib
or bed, only bookshelves and an armoire. Children don't sleep
here anymore, but they've left their imprint here nonetheless.

My bath was quick so I'd have time to prepare for Ellie's
arrival. I could make the macaroni and cheese tomorrow, but
I needed to gather materials for her first. I went up in the
attic, pulled the chain to the light, and surveyed the landscape
of sheet-covered furniture, vinyl wardrobes, leather trunks,
and boxes. The topography of the past. On my left were the
dark brown ones, from my mother, stacked four deep; the
smaller black one from Theo's family, and farther away, on
the right, the green ones Theo and I had packed with the
children's things. I knelt in front of Theo's black family trunk
and ran my hand across its dusty lid. A chimney fire at his
parents' Wilmington estate destroyed everything in their attic,

the second floor, and most of the first; only a few scrapbooks and yearbooks from the library had been retrieved. I'd forgotten how little remained from Theo's side, and I felt a sudden tenderness toward it now, as if it were an urn, or a small casket of bones. The Harris luggage tag dangled from the right-side handle, and I cupped it in my hand. When his parents sold the main property and moved into the carriage house, there wasn't room for too many old memories, anyway; it was as if the fire conspired in their downsizing. But unlike my mother, they had at least lost their money the old-fashioned way: in a stock market crash.

I sighed and turned to my family's trunks. Between my mother's family, the Biddles, and my father's, the Stinsons, I had dozens of leather-bound albums stashed inside, each embossed with the family crest. As I get older, I understand the practicality of monogramming—so useful for those with a flagging memory. Once I was at bridge club and couldn't for the life of me remember my host's first name. The hand towels in the bathroom saved me: *M* was for Mary. Of course!

I pulled out book after book and started to leaf through them. I'd have to pick and choose what would be useful to Ellie so as not to overwhelm her. My father's African safari, for instance, with the bloody zebra carcasses, was probably something to avoid. She might, however, be interested in my aunt Lillian's time as a missionary in Costa Rica. (We told people she was a missionary, but what she really did was give family money to young men she found attractive and compelling. "He speaks like a poet!" she'd told us one Christmas, and while my mother smiled tersely, my darling aunt Caro replied, "And have you played with his pentameter yet?")

But choosing a topic? That was harder. Ellie's teacher wanted the class to gather materials on an "aspect" of the family—a sport or a hobby that was threaded through the generations. *Interview a grandparent and focus on one aspect of the family,* was what the assignment sheet said. *Collect items for scrapbook pages and write one or two paragraphs about this aspect.* She read it to me over the phone, and her voice changed when she read it, in a serious, concentrating way.

"I think we should do cooking," Ellie said.

I loved the way she said "we," as if I were her classmate, but I had to stifle a bit of laughter as I informed her that neither of her great-grandmothers knew how to boil water.

"What about the great-grandfathers?"

This swelled me with pride for her father's unique cooking abilities. I had taught him how to make a *croque monsieur* at ten, and by the time he was in high school, instead of taking his prom date to the country club for dinner, he made her steak on our patio. Tom, I was certain, packed his own lunch.

"Well, men didn't cook much back then, dear. They worked and traveled a lot."

"So there are no family recipes?" she asked innocently.

"Not really," I sighed.

She thought about this for a moment; you could feel the heat of her brain absorbing this new information, this *lacking*. Recipes could fill up many pages of a report. Cooking was an excellent choice when you were going for quantity.

"Did they eat a lot of takeout?"

"Yes," I said and smiled, and left it at that. Let one of her other privileged Main Line classmates be the one to stand up and say her family had servants who planned seasonal menus, who shopped, cooked, and cleaned up after them. That her family recipes included Mamie's buttermilk pancakes.

Her disappointment was palpable, even over the phone. She'd imagined photos of her grandmother and great-grandmother in the kitchen, heads bowed over a marble rolling pin. She'd hoped for photographs of birthday cakes, of glistening roasts, of generations gathered around the barbecue pit. She'd hoped, in short, for another family. I told her I thought a lot of other children would choose "Family Recipes"; that if she wanted to stand out, she'd have to think of something cleverer anyway.

"But I already drew the cover," she confessed.

I laughed, and she giggled, too, realizing how silly and futile a decision that was. I decided to let Tinsley handle the rest of that conversation—about being organized but also being flexible. Applauding the cover before it was thrown away. A mother's place, not a grandmother's. Still, I glistened with a mother's pride as I held the phone—that some part of me had resulted in a child who could see a project complete, whole and pleasing, before she'd even begun.

I sat on the attic floor paging through the scrapbooks, looking for "aspects." There were no common sports—some played tennis, some golf. Some rode animals and some hunted them, like my father. (My great-grandfather Biddle and his brother were alcoholics, but I didn't think a family recipe like shaken martinis would go over so well.) There wasn't even a common town—we'd scattered. Some lived in Chestnut Hill and Connecticut, in addition to the Main Line. And Theo's family was from Wilmington of course.

Gardening? There was a photo of my father and me cross-legged on the path, fiddling near the stone wall past the patio. We must have been working on our fairy garden. I remember how gently he gathered toadstools and wove lean-tos of grass with moss roofs, while I assembled a family of pine-cone mice. We made a new one every year, until I was sixteen and stopped speaking to him. I'd tried to get Tom interested in building one, but he preferred large projects—he loved digging, carrying rocks, getting dirty. Even as a little boy, he thought big, and had no patience for anything too twee. But Ellie—perhaps she'd enjoy it? It was possible she was too old, and had already passed through her magical phase. I'd have to ask her come spring.

I turned the pages. All the family homes featured beautiful gardens, especially my mother's first "rose cottage" in Nantucket, before it was sold to pay taxes. I ran my hand over the photo, feeling the warmth and minerals and salty air that combined to make that corner of the island magical enough to allow roses to climb up walls. I remember how much it hurt my mother to give it up, how she cried over it twice; once when she sold it, and once, years later, in her hospital bed, knowing she'd never go there again. That was the last thing she wanted to see, imprinted on her for eternity: pink roses and blue sky. It proved as ephemeral as the fairy garden, though, didn't it, Daddy?

That little garden started a lifelong love of flowers and plants, though, so I suppose I should thank my dear departed dad. I fill my own flower boxes, plant my own bulbs, pull my own weeds, but I know none of the other women in my family had ever actually touched soil. (Or diapers, or dishwater, for that matter.) My mother creamed her hands and slept with cotton gloves on; she even wore gloves when she drove a car, as if to protect her hands from leather. When she died and they folded her hands across her chest in the casket, they still looked alive, as if they could reach out suddenly and touch me across the cheek.

No, "Gardening" was probably not destined to be Ellie's "aspect," either. After several hours of searching, the best common theme I could come up with was "Architecture." Two architects in the family, after all—my father and Theo—and every house in every photo elegant and grand. Even mine, so leaky and imperfect, so inappropriate for old age with its sets of steep stairs—even mine has the high tin ceilings, the deep windowsills, the three miniature fireplaces Theo was so proud of. We are a people, all of us, who love the great bones of a house. Even when it's drafty and expensive to heat. Even when it sits on the auction block. The last year of my mother's life, I would sit with her in her little room, me in the armchair, and she on one edge of the bed, working the trim of the matelasse coverlet between two fingers like a talisman. Suddenly, she'd stand up and walk over to the dresser, pick up her silver mirror or brush, then stop, one hand in the air, and spin around. "Where's the drawing room?" she'd cry. "Where is the foyer?" She looked at me the way children have looked at parents since the beginning of time. Expectantly. Assuming I would know the answer to even an unanswerable question.

"That's in the other house, Mother. This is your pied-à-terre."

"Ah," she'd say, and smile, lulled by the information, or merely soothed by the sound of foreign words.

Architecture; that would be my recommendation. The cover, I thought, would be easy for Ellie to redraw. A door perhaps, or a charming door knocker. Why, I could give her all of Theo's old blueprints to use! They were in one of the dark trunks, I think.

When I reached the attic stairs, the momentum of the creaking floor sent the light cord swinging slightly over my head. I could feel the breeze on my scalp as my eyes landed briefly on the green trunks in the corner, the ones I didn't dare open.

I turned off the light, climbed back down, and went to bed, much as Ellie must have the evening before, thinking I had it all planned out.

Ellie was still in her Langley uniform when she arrived, carrying a canvas bag as if she knew she'd be taking things home. Tinsley didn't come in, but watched and waved to me through the car window, as if she was in a huge hurry to be somewhere else. Though a welcome change—I would endure no questions about sodium content of foods or whether I planned to screen a PG-13 movie—this was unusual, completely unlike her, and it struck me enough to note it here.

We sat in the dining room, where I'd already spread out the scrapbooks, and arranged the macaroni and cheese casserole, plates and forks, and tea sandwiches I'd made. Nothing too fancy; nothing that would damage our artifacts or distract us from our task. She started with a small, polite serving of macaroni and cheese. It looked different to her, I'm sure, with its toasted bread crumbs and curly noodles. She took one tentative bite, then stood up to ladle more onto her Beatrix Potter plate. After that was gone, she chose a round sandwich and examined it in the air before she ate it, as if trying to determine how it had been shaped. Only after she'd chewed and swallowed it did she ask if I'd used a cookie cutter on the bread, and I told her it was a shot glass.

"A shot glass?" She wrinkled her nose, and I brought her one from the kitchen.

"This is a shot glass," I said. "The edges don't need to be sharp to cut the bread."

She held it in her hand. "Well, it seems too small to drink out of, so you may as well use it for something," she said, and I smiled. I was learning—she was practical, she liked jelly, she liked cheese, and she took her homework very, very seriously.

I suggested we look through the scrapbooks together, and perhaps a theme would emerge. She opened the first one and asked the usual kinds of questions—"Who is that?" and "Where are they?" and "When was this taken?" I took care to point out the large homes in the backgrounds. About halfway through the second scrapbook she asked me if I'd looked at them earlier in the day.

"I looked at them last night, before I took them down from the attic. Why?"

"Because you're not really looking, you're just waiting for me to look."

"Well, I've seen them before," I said defensively.

But she was right. I *was* waiting; my moment would come in just a few pages.

But when Ellie turned the page and saw a photo of my father looking at blueprints, she barely gave it a glance. She was more interested in the photo opposite it, an eight-by-ten of my mother on a horse, posing with a shotgun.

"You know, that photo gives me an idea," I said.

"Guns?" she said. "I don't think Ms. Westerman wou—"

"No, the other one. The blueprints. My father was an architect and so was Grandpa Theo. And there are so many beautiful homes in all these pictures. Nantucket, Bar Harbour, Stamford, the Adirondacks . . . and did you see my uncle's house in Miami Beach?"

"Um—"

So what do you think of 'Architecture' as a theme?"

"Aspect."

"Yes, well, aspect then."

"I don't know, Grandma," she said, wrinkling her nose. "It's so . . . grown up."

"Well, cooking was also grown up."

She shrugged. "But kids *can* cook. If they want to."

I wanted to say they could also build houses, of a sort. Lincoln logs and whatnot. Even my fairy garden contained structures. But it was a lame argument; she'd won. I'm a little ashamed to admit I felt deflated.

"Well," I said brightly, "if we don't think of anything else, we know 'Architecture' will certainly work. It can be your fallback."

She continued to turn pages, still scanning the photos earnestly. But there was a detachment about the way she did it that reminded me of dealers at flea markets. All business. It was clear my idea had been shot down—you could tell by her posture and the little furrow of blond hair between her eyebrows. She wasn't going to change her mind. It was a boy's quality, really, that kind of focus. Tom had it, too. He had his choice of clients at the law firm, and he always chose the ones who were innocent. Tinsley says it's a gift, his ability to know what's in a person. To sort through the rubble of an organizational chart and find who is destined to rise to the top. He could probably choose presidential candidates, she once said, be a political consultant. And now, watching Ellie, perhaps she could, too. She certainly was looking through the scrapbooks with nation-building intensity. Then it struck me with a smile: this was also how Theo looked at his blueprints.

"Is this your father, here?" she asked, lingering on a page.

I nodded. It was a snapshot of him in the Adirondacks, submerged in the lake up to his chin. Behind him in the water, perhaps thirty feet away, were two ducks. But all I saw when I looked at it was the "cabin" on the lake, a compound really, with tennis courts and a boathouse, that Mother had been forced to sell. I'd planned to take my girlfriends for a weekend there just after high school graduation; the invitations were sent, the menu was chosen, and poof, it had to be canceled. When I called my father to beg him to stop, his secretary said he was out of the country and couldn't be reached. I took the train downtown and sat at a coffee shop across from his office, waiting for him to walk out the door, waiting for a new lie to unfold. But he never showed up.

"Are you thinking 'Swimming'?" I asked. There was a lot of water in the vacation photos. Perhaps that could be a common sport.

"No," she sighed as she turned the page. "I just like the picture."

I prattled on a bit, about how clear and cold that lake was, and how the children slept in the boathouse and watched the ducks until it grew dark; how entire families used to canoe to the country club for dinner, dressed in black tie and bare feet. Tuxedos in a canoe, Ellie, can you imagine that! Then I stopped myself. What was I doing, trying to make her yearn for another version of something I couldn't give her? The family cabin, the yearly treks, the dinners of fresh-caught trout under the moose head in the dining room. The skating parties in the woods overlooking the pond, catered bonfires with hot Mexican cocoa. She would never have that childhood. That's what my father had taken away—not just the ease of life but the yearly rituals, the boisterous vacations in an assortment of wonderful places, the big houses overflowing with family and friends, the fresh maple syrup in winter and the cod cakes and eggs for breakfast. These things were sold to strangers to pay taxes.

I went to the kitchen and brought out the cookies I'd made. Nothing fancy, just fork-pressed sugar cookies with pink sprinkles since it was near Valentine's Day, but I'd baked them on parchment paper, as the magazine suggested, and they'd come out perfectly, not the least bit burned on the bottom. I was proud of how well I cooked; I'd taught myself. After the houses were sold and Mother moved to Aunt Caro's carriage house, I went to Bryn Mawr College, as planned, but with no walking-around money and no understanding of what one could do with a hot plate. I started small, with cocoa, trying to replicate the wonderful flavor of those ice-skating parties in the woods. I cut up real chocolate, learned to whip cream, bought a grater for the cinnamon stick. A simple thing, but done well. From there I moved on to French toast, *croque monsieurs*. It was years before I graduated to the inside of an oven; I found roasts terrifying. But I learned. I persevered. And Mother, well, her friends fed her. She went from being the consummate hostess to the consummate guest, overnight.

The cookies smelled sweet and buttery, but Ellie didn't

look up from the page, not even when I set the plate down under her nose.

I looked up at the clock, fiddled with the hem of my sweater, edged the cookie plate even closer to her.

"Anything strike you?"

"Not yet," she said, without looking up.

"Shall we just skip to the ones of me, as a little girl? Maybe that would be less grown up, as you put it."

"No," she said. "I'd rather just go in chronological order."

The word sounded heavy in her mouth, as if it were the first time she'd said it, a vocabulary word.

Minutes passed, pages turned. She ate one cookie distractedly as she viewed the scrapbook; she seemed to appreciate neither. I took away the dishes, rinsed them, came back. Cleared my throat, looked around my own living room. Two formal paintings of dogs looked down on us from the mantel. We'd never had a pet, since our yard was so small. But my mother loved dogs—we had three Labradors at the main house—and Theo's family, as I recall, kept beagles.

"What about 'Pets'?" I asked.

"I don't see any pictures of them."

I frowned. "There's bound to be some."

"Not yet."

"Or . . . 'Art,'" I said too brightly. "There's beautiful art in many of the homes."

"Was anyone in your family a painter?"

"Well . . . no."

She nodded as if the matter was settled.

Another half hour passed. I took to flipping through *National Geographic*s and *Ladies' Home Journal*s, looking for random ideas and calling out one or two—"Playing Cards"? "Fashion"?—before stopping completely, realizing the futility.

"I don't think this is going to get solved tonight," Ellie said. Something in the way she said it, and the way she'd been nodding quietly, reminded me of a psychiatrist. I frowned and picked at a pill on my velvet armchair.

I stood up. I was happy to end the evening—the one I'd envisioned as a quilting bee, and that had started to feel like an IRS audit.

"Sometimes it's best to sleep on things, dear," I said.

She asked to take a few scrapbooks home, and I hesitated. She said she'd take good care of them and I nodded; I knew she would. I also knew that taking them home meant taking away my influence; she would look over them with her mother. Tinsley, a darling girl really, but one who knew nothing about me or my family, would suggest unusual aspects to her; Tinsley would see something different in the pages than I would, than Theo, than Tom. And what if Tinsley started asking questions, dredging up things? She had always been such a curious person, that was one of the things Theo and I had loved about her. When we shared a meal, she never failed to inquire after Theo's business or our tennis games, our tomato plants, what-have-you. If you had a new sofa she would ask where you had it made, and what kind of fabric it was. What questions would she carry forth into that scrapbook? There were no pictures of my daughter—I purposely hadn't even opened that trunk. But what if she started in on my father, my mother? The last thing I could imagine doing was explaining our family's heartaches to Tinsley. The very thought of it made me feel queasy. Funny, isn't it, that I could sooner imagine telling Ellie? A child over an adult!

"Well . . . as long as you're careful," I said finally. "And remember, there's more to look through here, upstairs. Don't make any . . . snap decisions."

I put them in her tote bag and we sat on the window seat together, watching for the lights of Tinsley's station wagon. When it was 8:15 and she still hadn't arrived, I dialed her cell phone number but it went to voice mail. She was one of those people who insisted you leave a "brief message," so I simply said, "Tinsley, your daughter is wondering where you are."

"She never answers her phone," Ellie said quietly.

I looked over at Ellie but her eyes were fixed on the floor.

"Well, that seems silly, doesn't it? Why have one?"

"And she never lets me play games on it, either."

"She probably thinks those games are a waste of time. And they *are*." Tinsley had excellent policies, I thought, on some of these things. No video games ever. No television on a school night. Good, solid parenting, that.

"She gets mad if I even touch it." Ellie's eyes were fixed on the floor. "You know, when it rings or something. She freaks out."

I patted Ellie's hand.

"Someday you'll have your own phone, and maybe you won't let *her* play games on it."

She smiled. "Even if she begs."

Across the street a young woman was walking two dogs on one leash. "Dogs," I thought—I was seeing everything in "aspects." A group of college boys passed her but didn't whistle or hoot; it was too early in the evening for that. Ellie sat with one leg tucked under her, looking out at the street, watching the dogs and boys, waiting for the next thing to happen, while I waited for the next thing she would tell me. I couldn't force it. I just had to let it come.

May 27, 1967

regular bath
leftover oatmeal

THEO DIDN'T COME HOME LAST night. Looks a tad dramatic when I write it down, doesn't it? But it isn't, I know in my bones.

Yes, it happens to be one year to the day after my high school reunion, but I don't entertain thoughts of Theo's retaliation, or of my comeuppance. Perhaps if I felt guiltier I would. Perhaps if he knew of my transgression I would. When I think back on that night, it felt necessary and absolute. There could have been no other ending. The Tuesday before, Emma ran a fever so high I woke Theo and asked him to drive us to the emergency room. He rubbed his eyes and looked at his watch. He said he'd only come to bed an hour earlier. What? I'd said as I held Emma tightly, though I hadn't misheard him. He didn't repeat himself, he only blinked and sat still, as if his eyes were trying to adjust to the darkness. I told him to get dressed and meet me downstairs, and he asked me if I wasn't overreacting. Children get fevers, he said. Get dressed, Theo, I replied.

At the hospital, they decided to keep Emma overnight for observation. Thought it was just a virus, but they wanted to be safe. I asked the nurse if she could roll a cot into the

room, and she turned to us and asked if we wanted one cot
or two. One, I said.

No, I'm certain it was work keeping Theo at the office.
"All-nighters" are part of any young architect's life (thirty
being young for an architect, yet old for a mother). He had
stayed over several times before, so it didn't even register
as an important detail. The trains stop running at 10:30,
and there are sofas in nearly everyone's office. It was common practice and all the wives knew it. I confess I didn't
even notice his absence until morning—the baby slept
through the night, finally, and so did I. It was only at 5 a.m.
when Emma tumbled in and announced she'd had a bad
dream that I told her Daddy would take her back to bed and
she informed me, half shouting, half sobbing, that Daddy
wasn't there!

That's what aggravated me: not that he might be cheating on me, or lying about his whereabouts, but that he
couldn't deal with Emma. I groaned as I stood and scooped
her up. She was big for three and a half, and loud. She snuf-
fled in my arms, wiping her nose with her hand. I always
thought of girls as quiet, because I was that way—witty,
perhaps, but not boisterous. My mother says Emma takes
after her sister Caroline, which gives me hope: we all love
Aunt Caro, who arrives at staid family events with water
balloons and firecrackers smuggled in from her drives to
and from Kentucky, where she keeps horses. My mother
used to say she looked like she was full of secrets, but
always willing to let you in on one. Emma has her coloring, too; darker than my mother and I, almost black Irish

looking, with Theo's turquoise eyes. You never know what you're going to get in the stew of the womb. But when I wished things for Emma, and tried to imagine her future unfolding, I wished for a spirit, and a life, like Aunt Caro's. Tomboy spunk in a beautiful package—that's what I told myself my daughter was heading for. She was just taking her time getting there.

I cradled her head with one hand, and her thick dark hair, always a challenge, felt even more tangled than usual, and she smelled of oil and dust, that vague place between dirty and clean. She often smelled that way. Even as an infant, even after I bathed her, a few hours later something greasy would emanate from her again. I'd say to Theo, she just doesn't smell like she's supposed to, and he'd look at me like I had two heads. People would go on and on about the glorious smell of a baby's scalp; other mothers buried themselves in the furry intersection at the base of their child's neck, and I kept asking my pediatrician if she had a skin condition, allergies, or clogged sweat glands. Every baby is different, he said. Every sense of smell is different.

My mother said some babies simply have oily scalps, just like adults. My pediatrician suggests a different shampoo, and that does seem to help. But when I ask my mother what I smelled like as a baby, she rubs her hand across my cheek, says I was sweeter than any angel, then changes the subject. She does that often, gives a compliment that doesn't really answer the question. I think she doesn't want to admit that she rarely bathed me herself; Louise did. Whenever I ask her a question about parenting, she often struggles to put an answer together. That's what having servants will do to you, I suppose.

Late at night I'd sneak in to watch Emma sleeping, elegant and quiet, even after a bad day. She looked so sweet in her bed, so calm. I'd breathe deeply in her room, more filled with the cotton candy smell of baby lotion than with her. But now, with the baby and his greedy cries, I was too tired to do anything but Emma's basic maintenance. Too tired for watching her breathe in her sleep, too tired for guilt or overcompensation. I crouched over Emma's pink bed, my back protesting as I tried to place her gently down in the middle, between her bunny and her teddy bear, where there was still an indentation on the covers. But my aim was off, and her cheek rolled against her bunny and she cried, "Ow, my eye, my eye!" Since the bunny was soft, plush as a mink coat, I couldn't imagine she was doing anything but exaggerating.

"Oh, please, Emma. Your eye is fine," I said.

"The whiskers!" she wailed. "The whiskers!"

Was it possible the bunny's fine nylon whiskers, as thin as hair, had actually poked her in the eye as I lowered her down? I pulled her hand away to look; her eye wasn't even red.

"Emma, you're fine," I said more firmly.

"I'm not fine! I'm not fine!"

My breasts seized up, tingling, preparing to nurse, as they sometimes did when she cried, not just her brother. It had shocked me the first time it happened; made me understand why mothers in Europe breast-fed toddlers: because their breasts told them to. I squeezed my arm against it, willing it to stop. For it all to stop, really. I tightened the strap on that side of my bra for more support. I would never be one of those hippies who burned her bras; I needed mine more than ever.

I don't know how long I watched her flail on her bed. Ten seconds? Enough. Enough to see her pound her fists into her pastel chenille spread, hard enough to raise dust. I left her mid-tantrum, closing the door to her small room, and to the baby's room. If she wakes him up, I thought, I'll kill her.

"We can talk about this when you're calm," I called to her from the other side of the door.

She pounded her fists against the door, shrieking louder, and a few seconds later I heard the baby crying in his crib. I closed my eyes and counted to ten, willing him to stop, or her to stop; neither one did. Guilt seeped from my heart into my limbs. Two sobbing children, and it wasn't even daylight.

I stood up and went to the baby's room and put his pacifier back in his mouth and turned on his music mobile, hoping he'd go back to sleep, hoping he didn't want to nurse.

I backed out of his room slowly and nearly stepped on Emma, in the hallway.

"Ow!" she cried and I winced, expecting the baby's cry. I closed his door swiftly.

"Emma, what is wrong with you this morning?" I whispered.

"That bunny made me mad."

"Well, should we put the bunny in the naughty chair?"

"No, I forgave him."

"Then . . . ," I sighed, "then I forgive you for waking up your brother." I hesitated a moment and then added, "Do you want to come help me in the garden later this morning? We could find some worms, we could—"

"No," she said. "The garden is dumb."

And the moment, the crack in the armor, is gone.

Later, Betsy would point out that the tantrum was all Theo's fault. We laughed at all the different ways Betsy could absolve me and blame Theo. Theo's fault for never being home. Theo's fault for not making enough money to have servants. Theo's fault for the genes that combined with mine to make Emma just a bit different from the child we saw in our minds, the photograph of a life, the one you hope for, plan for. Not the one you have. But when I thought of my married life, the picket fence, the Christmas photos with children dressed in red velvet, I never thought there would be a shadow behind my husband, of another man.

My high school reunion was a bit like being trapped in the world's longest receiving line. So many people I half knew. My old lab partner, Bill Miller. Lou Ann Banner, whose locker was next to mine for four years. It was as if there were two of me: one who hugged each of them, and one who scanned the room for Peter over their shoulders. He was there, I just knew it. I imagined him hiding behind a nest of emerald balloons, peeking around the wide bass of the jazz trio, cloaked in the camouflage of a blue blazer. At most Main Line parties you couldn't tell the men apart from the back, but I was certain I would know Peter right away. Certain he wasn't one of the pairs of flannel shoulders I watched heaving with laughter. I nibbled on a cracker with cucumber and pimiento and watched the band. It was one of those earnest groups where the men nod and sway and make faces when they play. No one was dancing yet; it was too early, people had too much to say and not enough to drink.

I saw Peter before he saw me. He was making his way across the crowded gym, weaving gracefully between hanging streamers and swaying people, pausing for nods and handshakes along his route. Halfway through, his eyes found mine and held.

"Annie," he said and smiled, covering the last few yards in double time. His hands were on my hands, and his lips were against my cheek, lingering there a moment too long, as if they were just scouting out the territory for later. "It's been ages."

"I was hoping you might make the trip."

"Oh, we live here now."

My face flushed, and I wasn't sure if it was fear of his proximity, or the heavy width of the word "we."

"Really? Since when?"

"Last month."

We exchanged basic information: where we lived, how many children. He mentioned that his wife was from Baltimore and didn't feel at home here yet.

"Is she here? I'd love to meet her."

"She stayed back; one of the kids is sick."

"Oh, mine was sick earlier this week. Terrible fever."

"But you weren't?"

"Me?"

"Sick, you weren't sick?"

"No, no. Why, do I look . . . unwell?"

His eyes skimmed my body lightly before landing back on my face. "I didn't think it was possible, but you look better than you did in high school."

"I look old."

"No, you look . . . wise."

"Wise to your tricks, maybe," I said and we both laughed.

He looked toward the punch bowl. "And what about you? Is your illustrious architect husband getting you a drink?"

"He's at a ribbon cutting."

"Oh, of one of his skyscrapers?"

"One of his shopping malls, actually. But I'll tell him you find him illustrious."

He laughed, and I watched him, marveling at his wide, easy smile as if it had been a dozen years since I'd seen teeth.

"Do you, too?"

"Do I what, Peter?"

"Find him illustrious?"

I narrowed one eye, considering this. I wasn't used to hanging adjectives on Theo, but if I had to choose one, that would not be it. Industrious, perhaps. He'd had the nerve to be upset that I wouldn't go with him instead of to the reunion. He'd said I lived a mile from Langley, and anyone I wanted to see I could probably see at the grocery store. He said I didn't care about his work. I said he didn't care about my friends. Both of us were right, and we knew it. I stopped short of adding that he didn't care about his own daughter when she was sick.

"So . . . couldn't someone else have cut the ribbon, Annie? Or does he have special scissors?" Peter teased.

"I didn't come here to talk about my husband," I said with a smile.

February 20, 2010

Today was the indoor doubles round-robin, and as usual, I'm sore. If I'd played singles, I probably would have needed an ambulance. Betsy and I laughed about this tonight on the phone: why does anyone consider tennis a "life sport"? It's desperately hard on the knees, elbows, shoulders. It's a sweaty game played on hot, humid days. It's a young person's game if ever one was invented. But no, we're encouraged to play it for life, which I have, mostly, except when the babies were little. Theo played every Saturday morning throughout our marriage, though never with me. He played until he collapsed on the court, clutching his chest, crying out to his partner, Bix, as if protesting a foot fault. Life sport, indeed. I remember whispering that very thing to Tom at Theo's funeral. Theo's friends all gave eulogies that wove in tennis stories, tennis metaphors. Bix insisted on tucking a tennis ball into the casket. I leaned over and groaned, "Life sport, indeed," to Tom, and he pointed out that he was sure all that tennis at least helped the pallbearers with their heavy lifting. We giggled, and I saw a slice of Tinsley's furrowed brow coming over Tom's shoulder. Then it was gone, and it was as if she wasn't even there.

On the court next to us were four women Tinsley's age

who ran and lunged and grunted as they swung their tan, fit arms. Even when they were finished and put on their sweaters, you could see the outlines of their muscles pushing through the cable pattern, distorting it. One of them saw me watching her and smiled back sweetly, as if catching me in reverie for how I used to look. But no, I wasn't in thrall; I was wondering if I'd pegged her right, if she was the kind of woman who wore her tennis dress everywhere, to the market or a parent-teacher conference. Tinsley was becoming like that, I'd noticed; always dressed in warm-ups, looking like she was going to, or coming from, something sweaty.

When I returned home, I soaked in Epsom salts, and as soon as I got out of the tub, Tinsley called to ask if Ellie could come tonight instead of Saturday and I said certainly, of course.

"Whatever happened to you the other night?" I asked.

"What do you mean?"

"You were nearly an hour late picking up Ellie."

"Oh, Ann, I told you I wouldn't be there until close to nine."

"You did not," I said, but my voice wavered. Might she have?

"Sure, I did. We're going to have to get you a BlackBerry, Ann, to keep track of your appointments."

I shuddered at the thought.

"Anyway, Ellie's very excited to tell you her new theme."

"Oh, she found one, did she?"

"How could you not? That was a treasure trove of material. And I imagine I haven't seen the half of it."

"Did you . . ." The words caught in my throat. ". . . help her? At all?"

"God no. She rejects all my ideas out of hand."

I smiled. "She knows what she's after, I suppose. You're like that, too, dear."

"Am I?"

"I think so. You had no trouble decorating your house, or choosing china. I remember how I struggled when I was a young bride. Not you."

"Well, Ellie's a lot like Tom, too. Speaking of which, he'll drop her off, okay?"

When Tom and Ellie arrived at seven that night, he looked exhausted, and I told him so, in no uncertain terms. He said he'd worked late all week on a big case, and I frowned. I hated the thought of Tom working himself into the ground, like Theo. He hunched his shoulders, making himself small, as if he didn't fit, and was suddenly uncomfortable in the home he'd grown up in.

Ellie hung up her coat and carried her tote bag to the dining room table, where I'd set out a plate of pigs in blankets from the farmers' market, along with ramekins of ketchup and mustard.

"People with a history of heart disease in the family shouldn't work so hard, Tom."

"I know, Mother."

"Your family needs you far more than any of your clients."

"Most clients don't even like me," he sighed. "I'm the one always forced to tell them the truth."

"Well, I like you," I said, patting his arm. "I'm sure you

deliver bad news exceedingly well." The first threads of gray were showing at his ears, and that made me feel older than any creak of my bones. That my children could be old. Were old.

"I like you, too, Daddy," Ellie called out from the next room.

"Thanks, sweetie," he said.

"What time should I come back for Ellie? Can't be too late. We have an ice-skating lesson in the morning. Dads and daughters."

"That sounds like good fun. I didn't know you still skated, Tom-o."

"Don't want to waste my skills since I learned from the best," he said, and I blushed with pride. I'd skated backward for a week, pulling his arms, urging him to move his legs one at a time. My back ached just remembering it. He did learn, and he stayed in figure skates with his old mother long enough to start skating backward, and then he heard the siren call of hockey. I drove him to the rink at 5 a.m. every Tuesday and Thursday for years, but I can't recall ever skating with him after that.

"Well, why don't I drop her at home later? You and Tinsley relax for a change."

"Oh, Tinsley won't be home. She's playing squash."

"At *night*?"

"Surely you've heard of electricity, Mother."

"Don't the two of you do anything in tandem?"

"Oh, you know Tinsley. She's got a schedule and she sticks to it."

"Yes, I suppose. But you need to have some fun once in a while. Let loose. Go dancing."

He did a quick tap dance on the floor and I laughed.

"Well," I said, "*you* relax then, sweetheart. I'll drop her at home."

"Are you sure?"

I nodded and told him I'd have Ellie home between 8:30 and 9:00. That's what I remember: 8:30 or 9:00.

Ellie ate the little hot dogs with great care—small bites, plenty of chewing. She used her napkin properly, to dab, not to wipe. Then she asked me if I was going to eat anything, and I recognized at once the combination of politeness and longing. I told her to go ahead, that I'd already eaten (and I *had* slipped two of them in my mouth while I was setting the table).

"So I did it," she said, after the last bite. "I didn't think I could but I did it."

"So you did. You finished them."

"No, Grandma, I mean I did the project—I found the aspect!"

"Really?" I put one hand against my mouth, feigning surprise. It wouldn't do to let her know that Tinsley had already filled me in.

"Yes! And I came up with the best one. One no one else will have!"

"What is it?"

"I'll show you," she said, and opened the green leather album.

She paged past photos of weddings, christenings, and parties. She breezed through the tall churches and the rolling backyards and the brocade tables, turning so fast they came together in a mosaic, silk dresses and stained glass and silver cocktails, pulpit and sandbox and seaside, marble and slate, sunlight and candlelight, low fog and bubbling champagne.

They ran together in my head the same way sometimes: the before taunting the after. Like watching a past life flash before your eyes. When my mother met me at Porter's Soda Shop and told me my father had left for good, and that she would be moving, the images started shifting then. Lining up in their flashing queue. I was furious with my father, and I didn't even know the real reason to be. My mother sat very still as I cried, only moving to take small sips of her root beer float. She seemed to have used up all her tears already, but now, I wonder, forget the sadness, where was her anger? Where was her fury? Finally, I took a sip of my own float, and my face went pale.

"Wait a minute, *you're* moving?" I said.

"Yes."

"Not 'we'?"

"Well, we're not a couple anymore. I have to get used to saying I."

"Mother, I meant me."

"Well, of course you're going to college, dear, in the fall. That much is certain."

"But what about on fall break, and Christmas and . . ."

"Well," she sighed, "I haven't quite worked that part out yet."

And the images of my other life began to pile up behind her. She smiled at me, a small smile, but not, I realize now, the kind of small smile that is all you can summon up, but the kind you are trying to contain. I imagine a fresh start might have seemed romantic to her then, at that moment, before the full realization of her financial ruin became clear.

I sighed and watched the pages of my life pass by again in Ellie's hands.

"Here!" she said breathlessly.

I leaned in. The photo she pointed to was small; the white corners that affixed it to the gray page were barely bigger than her fingernail. I squinted. It was a black and white of my father in his workroom, a separate cottage that sat nearly an acre away from the main house. He was always apart from us, my mother used to point out. Even before he left. I didn't understand what she was talking about—in my mind he was always at my side—or I was at his. If you extended every photo an inch in every direction, I imagined you'd find me lingering in every frame. In this shot, he was wearing a leather apron, smoking a cigar and laughing at whoever was behind the camera. Proof he was happy at that house at least once.

"Woodworking? Is that what you've chosen?" My father did love to tinker—he carved little boats for me and made drinks trays for Mother's friends. Of course, if my dear mother had been sitting next to me, she would have suggested "Philandering" as an aspect.

"You're getting warmer," she said and smiled. "Look at what he's making."

Behind his shoulder, on the edge of the sawhorse, I could make out a small roofline.

"Oh, a dollhouse!" I cried. "How perfect, Ellie! I'm sure every little girl in my family had one, if we look carefully. My father did make a marvelous one for me, I remember now, with a—"

She screwed up her face. "No, Grandma, it's not a doll-house."

"Well, surely—"

"It's a bird house."

"Bird house? I don't recall him ever making a bird—"

"Yes, he did. And if you look at this other picture, with the other people, there're two more in it."

She turned to a photo of my great-aunt Minna, standing with my mother in front of our first Nantucket cottage, the one that came from my mother's family. The roses climbing up the walls are so heavy and full I could almost smell them. My mother is perhaps twenty-five, already married, already a mother, yet at the height of her beauty. Her hair was so gold and fine, I used to expect butterflies to light on it. I held a finger up to the photo, as if I could feel it. When I needed hair for my fairy garden princess, I always used the fine strands from her hairbrush.

"No, over there." Ellie pointed impatiently. On my mother's left, two cedar-shake bird houses rose from the garden soil on sticks.

"Oh," I said.

"That's three, plus I have a bird house in my backyard . . . and you have one outside *your bathroom window*!"

My heart fell a story in my chest. How on earth had she seen that? I'd hung it in the tree so it was only visible, I thought, from a certain angle of the bathtub. The green base and brown roof blended in with the foliage. Or so I'd thought.

"Grandma?"

"Yes?"

"You seem a million miles away." It was one of her mother's expressions, wildly preferable to something glib her classmates might have said, like, "Earth to Grandma, do ya read me?"

"Do I? I'm just, uh, thinking about this idea of yours. This aspect."

"And?"

"I can't help thinking, Ellie, that dollhouses are . . ." I hesitated, wanting to choose the best words, "more family oriented, more historically significant, I think, than bird houses."

"No, Grandma. Dollhouses are too girly. And . . . I don't even like dolls."

"But a bird house is such a . . . I don't know . . . such a small thing. In the scheme of a family and a heritage and a . . . legacy." I tasted tears in my throat. Were they caused by her choice, or my own fumbling words? She knew nothing, so why did it matter, why did it hurt so much? I breathed in sharply, willing it away. I was becoming a dreaded thing: a silly, sentimental, forgetful old woman.

"But, Grandma," she said, rising to her knees with excitement, "I could buy a silk bird and wire it to the cover!"

She had me. How could anyone argue against such a brilliant book cover?

I cleared my throat, shook off whatever had welled up. "I believe our Adirondack house had a bird house out back," I said with a smile, and we spent the rest of the evening flipping the pages quickly and carelessly until we found it. By the time we made a list of everyone in the photos, names and ages and other pertinent information, it was nearly nine. I told her we could work on the cover next time.

I drove Ellie home and noticed that Tinsley's station wagon wasn't in the driveway. Tom rubbed his eyes as he stood at the door, and I worried that I'd woken him, that he'd fallen asleep at his desk.

"Sorry we're a bit late," I said.

He looked at his watch. "You're early, actually."

"Didn't we say eight-thirty?"

He blinked. "It's a weekend, so we said nine-thirty, Mom," he replied, with a softness at the edges of his voice. He reached out and squeezed my hand, and I let him, even though I knew what it meant and what he was trying to say and all I wanted was to yank my hand away and tell him, no, like a mother does, *you're wrong*.

I was on edge all the way home. I tried to keep my eyes on the road, and not think about my mother, and the day Aunt Caro called me from the carriage house to tell me someone had left the teakettle on all day, ruining the kettle and the stove, nearly setting fire to the whole kitchen. When Caro asked my mother how it had happened, how it could have gone unnoticed, she said she thought the kettle's whistle was a silly bird in the backyard. A few months later, we placed Mother in a nursing home. But this was different, I told myself. Dear lord, I may forget a time or a date now and then, but I know a pot from a bird!

I shook off the memory, but something lingered. I kept expecting a raccoon or a deer to leap into the path of my car; the wind to knock a tree across the road. I told myself Tom was just being gracious, not concerned. I told myself it was Ellie's project, not mine. But it didn't feel that way. No.

As much as Ellie and I had outlined and sketched, as much as we used innocuous tools like pencil and glue, I could feel the scraping at the earth beneath my feet, the trolling, the tilling. Dredging up things I didn't want to remember, but couldn't seem, somehow, to let go of.

March 4, 2010

"You're lucky," Betsy said, "that you didn't fall and kill yourself. Or god forbid, break a hip!"

If there were two words most frequently invoked for the purpose of spreading fear among older women, they had to be "broken hip."

Still, I laughed when she said this to me, fairly dancing at the mossy base of the tree I'd just shimmied out of.

"I used to climb trees much higher than this one," I said. "My house had fat sycamores lining the drive, which weren't good climbers, but out by the gazebo, there were oaks and maples and willows. I climbed trees every day when I was young," I said, brushing leaves from my shoulders.

"Have you looked in the mirror recently? You're not young anymore, Ann."

A sentence like that shouldn't sting between good friends, but that one did. Betsy had a knack for painful honesty. I faced her and raised one eyebrow. I was thinner and far stronger than she was, and it was obvious every time we played doubles. She wheezed on the court and squeezed her plump feet into her Tretorns. We were seventy-three but she looked seventy-five and I looked sixty-eight and we both knew it.

"It's not very tall for an oak," I said and Betsy rolled her eyes.

I looked up and smiled. The tree's spring shoots brushed across the butter-colored trim on the second story, leaving thin green streaks as it swayed in the wind. If the tree had been any wider, its branches would have encircled Theo's little deck upstairs, but it stopped just short. By summer the foliage would thicken, grow lush, and conveniently shade the slate patio below.

"What were you doing up there, anyway?"

The bird house hadn't come willingly; I'd yanked on the twine for nearly five minutes, angry with myself for not bringing scissors. But climbing a tree with a sharp object seemed unduly risky, even to me. Finally it gave way and tumbled out of my fingers, bringing small bits of branches and the rhythmic *ping* of acorns with it as it crashed on the patio. It sat there now, behind us, mostly intact except for its now-sideways chimney and the moss clinging to one side of the green enamel.

I brushed my hands together. "Taking down a bird house to photograph for one of Ellie's projects."

"That old chipped brown-and-green thing?"

I surveyed her curiously, surprised she'd ever noticed it, but not wanting the subject discussed. Maybe she'd merely glimpsed it when she walked up?

"Well," she deflected, "you could have bought her a nice new one at Firth's for nine dollars. Painted it any color you like. Red would be nice."

"It's an historical project."

"The historical preservation of Victorian bird houses?"

I laughed again. "Something like that."

"I never thought you, of all people, would turn out to be this sentimental." She sighed.

My heart skipped a beat; we'd never discussed the origins of that bird house. She couldn't know what it meant to me. Her comments, I told myself, simply referred to its obvious age. I swallowed hard and pressed my lips into a smile.

"I just like old things," I said.

"Uh-huh." She started toward her house. "Remind me to buy you a ladder for Christmas," she said as she left. "Or a handyman. I'll make sure he's old, since you like old things."

I picked up the bird house and dusted it off on my pants. I couldn't imagine it red or any color other than its own muted browns and greens. The moss that crept across it was lighter than the paint; it gave it a homey, cottagey look, as if a bird might actually live there, not just visit. The caramel-colored roof was steep; Theo would say it was too steep for its chimney. But bird houses didn't have to be brought up to code; they could be as rakish as a thrown-together fort. This one, despite the wild pitch of its roof and the lean of its chimney, had been assembled with love and care. I knew that much. I felt that pull again, of wanting to tell Betsy, but of course I didn't. Just as always. I'd learned over the years, the hard way, how different we were. How she always seemed to see those differences through a cloud of judgment, rather than the gauzy haze of empathy. I suppose I didn't want practical Betsy to know precisely how sentimental I could be.

In the kitchen I took a damp cloth and tried to clean the house over the sink. Sap clung stubbornly to parts of the brown slatted roof; it formed flat shellacky moles I'd have to chip away later with a tool. I pulled gently on the miniature rust-colored door and looked inside, fearing gummy waste, pecked walls. Assuming the birds had trashed their hotel room. But no, the finches and robins and cardinals had left it fairly clean. The wind and weather had beaten the bird house, not the birds.

What to tell Ellie of this? Could we sit with a book of North American birds, catalog the species and the behavior, tell her all I'd learned since the bird house went up? How in the beginning I watched them fly and flit from the comfort of my morning bath, before the children woke up, in those few weeks—was it a month? was it less?—before everything changed?

And how afterward I'd simply stand at the window, having come in to brush my teeth or cream my face or go through some other motion, and be surprised that it was still there, still standing and serving its purpose, providing a haven. All those days when Theo worked till dawn, the bird house swung in the breeze, less empty, less small and confining than my own dwelling.

Since I had to go out and run errands with Ellie, I took a shower to rinse the leaves from my hair, and at the last minute, I brought the bird house in with me, and let the hot water soak into its sticky roof.

When Ellie arrived, we hopped in the car and drove outside town to pick up supplies. Carole's Crafts was in one of the upscale strip malls Theo had designed. That was his legacy: a better strip mall. My father, who approved of me marrying an architect, would have been appalled by this. He worked only for people, not companies; he designed homes, not buildings. Theo didn't even design buildings, really, but places. Locales. He did make sure that all the stores had similar facades and similar signage—small, wooden, subtle. He was proud of how he made them blend in. But inside, where he'd had no control, all subtlety was lost—in Carole's Crafts, the aisles were crammed from floor to ceiling, boxes were open, displays pulled apart. People yakked on their cell phones as they searched through the rubble; one woman spoke in Russian over her receiver and I stared at her until she moved away.

"The nerve of people," I said as Ellie led me to the wreath-making area at the back of the store.

"They all have to call their kids because they're confused about what stuff to buy."

"Well, that makes sense."

"Here they are, Grandma!" she cried, and skipped to the shelf bulging with robins, cardinals, blue jays, finches, and ravens.

"What, no turkeys?"

"They only have those out for Thanksgiving, silly," she said and smiled. "We could come back then."

"Oh, I don't think there'll be a need for that," I said as a woman behind me shouted, "What size?" into her phone.

Ellie held up a cardinal in each hand, surveying them like a falconer. As she angled her head from one to the other, something about her bearing, the tilt of her chin and nose, was birdlike, too.

"Which cardinal do you like better?" she asked. "Blue eyes or black?"

"I rather like the blue jay," I said.

"No," she said with finality. "Red goes better with black-

and-white photos." She sounded exactly like Tinsley when she said it—firm and exacting but smiling. I remember the first time Tinsley cooked Thanksgiving dinner. I offered to bring a side dish, but she had all the recipes planned and a shopping list already made. Ellie and I left with the darker-eyed cardinal, foam board, and wire. Outside the magnetic door I dug my keys out of my handbag and asked if she wanted to go somewhere for ice cream.

"No, thanks. But—"

"But what?"

"Can we just go to the pet store and look? I promise I won't beg for a kitten or anything."

She pointed to the wooden sign a few doors away: SQUEAK'S PET VILLAGE.

"All right, why not?"

Some of the same people who'd been in the crafts store were also in the pet store, using their phones to photograph puppies. This looked ridiculous to me, snapping pictures with a phone. Like using a hand mixer as a microphone.

Ellie wiggled her fingers through the openings in a sheltie puppy's cage, despite the sign that said not to. She looked at me for a second, as if waiting for a reprimand, but I said nothing, just leaned down to marvel at how small the dog was and, indeed, how cute.

A few dogs later, Ellie headed toward the Kitten Korral and I lingered outside Aviary Avenue. I'd never cared much for parrots or macaws, which seemed more like clowns than birds. I preferred smaller birds: goldfinches, sparrows. A small brown bird in the cage suddenly burst into song and I nearly clapped my hands.

"Are you a nightingale?" I said.

"Nightingale," squawked the parrot.

"Look, Grandma, that little finch has only one leg."

I squinted. "Indeed she does."

She was smaller than the palm of Ellie's hand. We watched her hop from perch to perch, landing a bit unsteadily. Once she nearly fell off, but like a tightrope walker, quickly recovered.

"Her balance is off," I said quietly. "When you have only one of something, it affects your balance." I wrapped my arms around my ribs, and rubbed the spot where my right breast used to be. Gone, but never forgotten. Some nights I still dream of breast-feeding, the fullness and release, the smell in the air, as sweet as baked apples. When I wake up I am startled, and always, always hugging my chest, as if I was trying to rock myself back to sleep.

"Do you think she's a baby? That she was born that way?"

I pictured her in a pale blue shell, tumbling in the ovoid enclosure, scratching wildly for an exit, only one set of claws to break free of it.

"Probably not. Some things you are born with, and some things just . . . uh, develop."

We walked past rows of dog beds and collars, leashes and treats on our way out. So many ways a person could fritter away their money. Ellie asked me what my favorite animal was and I told her it was the emu. Hers, she confessed, was a koala.

In the parking lot I wondered about all the time Ellie and I had been spending together. Sooner or later we'd be at a

swimming pool, or I'd be in a robe. I'd bend over, or twist . . .
or worse, we'd be home, and she'd knock on the bathroom
door, and it would squeak open a few inches. I didn't want to
scare her with what she might see. I thought perhaps I should
tell her about my breast before she discovered it in some grotesque way, and I suddenly become her old, deformed shriv-
eled-up grandmother.

"I believe there's still time," I said brightly, "for a milk
shake or a float."

She said fine, and as we got in the car she cocked her
head and asked, "What's a float?" and I realized there was
work, so much work, to be done!

I headed to Stuart's, the only place I could think of where
she could have a root beer float and I could have a beer. Places
were so specialized now—you went to separate locations
for ice cream, for drinks, for food. Imagine driving to three
places when you used to walk to just one. The village of Bryn
Mawr wasn't as quaint as it had been when I went to college. Developers had found a way to commoditize its charm,
to make it look quaint instead of just being quaint. But it still
had Stuart's, a bar and grill near the train station that also
had a soda fountain and a spinning rack of greeting cards.
No matter that it sat next to a boutique that sold only jeans
and a restaurant that made only smoothies; one couldn't hope
for complete stagnation; one couldn't pine for everything that
had changed.

A handful of men around my age sat on stools, looking
as if they'd stopped off to have a few drinks and pick up
their wives' birthday cards. Familiar red baskets of glistening onion rings and French fries slid across the wooden bar

with a kind of grace impossible to find at a fast-food restaurant. There is more to inexpensive food than inexpensive ingredients; there has to be humility. Hardworking humility. I was comforted by the dirty aprons and dented spoons; they spoke of effort and toil. The muscles in the young woman's arm flexed as she scooped the ice cream for Ellie's float; anything good, anything worthy, I wanted to tell her, took some doing.

Ellie's eyes widened as the waitress set down my frosty glass.

"I'm only having one," I said, and she nodded.

There was plenty of time for me to drain the mug, and the waitress to refill it while Ellie was in the ladies' room lathering up her hands. It wasn't so much that in the surroundings of my youth I felt young; I was merely bolstering my courage for what I was about to tell her.

"Ellie," I said quietly when she came back, "do you know about breast cancer?"

"The pink ribbons," she said.

"I thought of this today when we saw that one-legged bird at the pet store, and I—well, do you know what breast cancer is? Do you know what it means, or, or, how you get it?"

"From . . . birds?" Her face was open and sincere, the opposite of scared. That's why I went on, I told myself. That's why.

"I had breast cancer," I said. "It means sometimes you have to have your breast removed."

"They cut it off?"

"Yes, that's what happened to me. Now I only have one breast. The left one. I wear a sort of pad to balance it out."

She tried not to look at my chest, but couldn't help herself. "How did that happen?"

"It's genetic. I had cancer and so did my mother and Aunt Lillian. You get it when you are born, when you are a tiny baby, and it shows up later."

"Will my dad get it, then?"

"No, honey, only girls need to worry."

"But you don't have any girls."

I blinked at her. I couldn't tell if she had missed the point or made one.

"Well, dear, I just wanted you to know. It's one of those interesting things about a person, like having a scar or a hidden constellation of freckles on your hip."

"Like Harry Potter's lightning bolt," she said.

"Yes," I said, relieved, and almost willing to believe that my ragged chest could be the source of such strength, such power, if only I was able to look at it in the proper way.

June 1, 1967

bubble bath
black coffee

PETER CALLED ME AFTER I dropped Emma off at nursery school. I was still shaking from my experience there, could barely register his voice.

I held the phone in one hand, the baby basket in the other. Don't cry, I said to the baby, to myself, to the air. Don't cry.

"Ann?"

I said nothing, but I know he could hear me, breathing, being, on the other end. I was aware of my own weight, the heaviness of a human being standing upright. It was unbearable, suddenly, and all I wanted was to fall into the pillow of his voice. The soft, appropriate words he always chose.

"When were you going to tell me, Ann?"

"When his draft number came up?" I answered feebly.

"Annie," he said. A world in one word. "Is he—"

"No," I said too quickly. "How did you know?"

"Is it a secret?"

"Well, no, of course not."

"I saw Betsy at the post office. She told me you'd had a boy this time."

"What did you say?"

"I asked her if you'd named him after me."

"Oh, Peter, you did not!"

"You're right. I did not."

He wanted to see me again, just for coffee. Not anything else, just coffee. Said he'd been thinking about me every day since the reunion. He said he was in my neighborhood for a business meeting and wondered if I could slip away. Just for coffee, Annie, I promise.

I said no. Although I hadn't seen him since that night at our class reunion, somewhere in the throat of that single syllable I knew there would be another chance, another meeting, another coffee. I was prescient; I was beginning to hear things people didn't say. I said I couldn't, but promised him I would call him next week, and he chuckled, saying he'd heard that one before.

"What do you mean?"

"I mean, when you broke up with me that August before college, when we met at your aunt's house, that's exactly what you said. Your parting words, for a dozen years."

"I broke up with you and then said I'd call you?"

"Well, it was a little worse than that. You broke up with me after I gave you three hundred dollars, and then said you'd call me."

"What?"

"Remember, your father had just left, and there was that business with the money? You were worried about going to college, about expenses, what you would wear. So I gave you a gift certificate to Lord and Taylor. You broke up with me two weeks later."

"I thought we both agreed to break up before college, and agreed to be friends."

"Ah, selective memory. You probably don't remember that on fall break, I ran into you with Mike Dunwoody and I cried like a baby right in front of you both."

"Who?"

He laughed. "See, he wasn't worth it! You broke my heart and you don't even remember him. Big, lanky guy with black hair, went to Evan Academy."

"Funny, I usually remember the big ones."

"Oh, that's choice," he laughed, "kick me in my weak spot." Peter was barely five ten, and everyone else in his family was taller. Even his mother was taller. "Maybe, Annie, you've had so many gentlemen you just can't possibly place them all."

"I think when you give birth, your brain goes fuzzy, and deletes the names of your past loves."

"Ah, the old fuzzy brain. See, you need coffee, and I know just where to procure it. It's kismet."

That was pure Peter—he had a way of convincing you that you needed the same things he did. I remember his chess club once held a car wash and, because I was on a diet, he convinced me that washing cars burned as many calories as calisthenics. Now that he was a journalist for the *Philadelphia Times*, this technique was probably how he convinced his sources to be interviewed—by showing them they needed the article written as much as he did. Your story needs to be told, I could practically hear him say. Let's do this together. Wasn't that what he said the night of the class reunion as he kissed me under the stars above the baseball diamond?—I know you want this as much as I do.

He was patient while I took a deep breath and explained

that I just wasn't up to seeing anyone, that I was still tired from giving birth, that I'd already had too much coffee and needed a nap, and that I would call him the following week, I really would, and he said that was fine, that he completely understood, which he didn't, of course, not really. He paused and I couldn't fill the space to help him understand, so I simply said good-bye. He didn't understand because he was a man and he didn't know what had just happened to me and I couldn't tell him. How do you tell what happened to someone who isn't a mother?

Emma had been fine at nursery school yesterday, fine. She'd run off toward the jungle mural and the macramé owls and monkeys with bright beaded eyes and never turned back. But today? Today she sobbed and lunged at me as I tried to leave, begging me to stay.

"Emma, it's time for you to go to school, and time for Mommy to go grocery shopping."

"I want to go with you!"

"No, honey, it's time for school."

She dropped to her knees and clawed at the hem of my capri pants, scraping her nails down my calf. "I hate you!" she said. "I hate the baby!"

The teacher extricated Emma's fingernails, one by one, from my leg. I can still feel them in me, like hooks; like shrapnel that lingers long after the war. Was this why some of Betsy's young babysitters wore those wide bell-bottomed pants? To protect their calves from thorns, rabid animals, and furious toddlers? The teacher cradled Emma and her straight hair fell around them both, blocking the light. She kissed her head, voluntarily, not because she was her mother, and when she looked up she mouthed, "She'll be fine."

I crept backward into the hallway, my guilt weighing me down, even though the baby was still in the car and my Kotex was about to overflow and I had every reason, every logical reason, to hurry. I thought it would be good for Emma, being with children her age, being away from the baby. And yes, part of me wanted a witness. Wanted the teacher to observe her and tell me whether she was normal, if this was indeed how girls nearly four years old behaved. Betsy had told me repeatedly that tantrums were normal, that sibling rivalry was normal. But who am I kidding? I thought the separation would be good for me. I thought it would be good for the baby. I thought it would help me bond with him instead of being irritated every time he cried or bit my sore swollen right breast.

In the car, the baby was asleep. I wiped the blood off my leg with a tissue, and drove home not thinking of Peter, or Theo, or any man, child, or other appendage. I thought of the preschool teacher.

I tried to memorize the serenity that lived in her hands and arms, the calmness and sweetness that came off her like incense as she enfolded my flailing, slippery daughter.

March 5, 2010

I was walking out the door, literally walking out the door with my tennis racket in hand, when I made the mistake of answering the phone. Tinsley's words sounded as if they'd been filtered through a wall of tears.

"Ann, I know you must have meant well, but . . . we really need to discuss what you told Ellie."

"Tinsley?" I asked dumbly. Was I stalling for time, or was I really surprised? Her voice seemed unusually deep, and there were several long stunned seconds when I believed, truly, that I had no idea who she was or what she was talking about.

"Yes, it's Tinsley, Ann, we need—"

"I'm afraid you've caught me on my way out—I, uh—"

"You need to explain this to me, Ann. What on earth made you tell a little girl she had the breast cancer gene?"

"That's certainly *not* what I told her."

"Well, that's what she *heard*."

I wrinkled my nose. Maybe that's what Tinsley heard. It was hard to believe that was Ellie's interpretation. She hadn't given any indication in that direction. None at all.

"Why, Ann? I don't understand."

"Well, the subject . . . just . . . presented itself."

I struggled to recall the exact context of our breast cancer discussion. I confess I could not. Later I looked up my diary entry to remind myself that it did, in fact, come up naturally. I wanted to show it to Tinsley as evidence, like a courtroom drawing.

"Well, how would that subject just come up, Ann? I don't—"

"Something . . . in the store prompted it, I believe."

"Did she touch your prosthetic, or—"

"Yes, something like that."

"I know she asks a lot of questions, but you can't give her too much information. It needs to be managed. Maybe you should have asked her to speak to m—"

"Ellie is very mature, Tinsley. She doesn't need to be mollycoddled."

"She was up all night, Ann! I think she was afraid she had cancer!"

I shifted my weight from foot to foot in my sneakers. I thought of the float we'd shared at Stuart's, the scoop bobbing in the fizz.

"Well, she did have a little cola with her ice cream. Maybe that kept her awake."

"You gave her *caffeine*?"

I sighed. Tinsley made it sound like I'd put a goddamn IV in her arm!

"No," I said firmly. "She drank a little cola, that's all. A few sips."

I couldn't wait to end the conversation so I could tell Betsy about it. Betsy, who had hated every girl her son ever dated. Over the years we'd raised eyebrows at their clothes and their

helmets of hair and their earnest fund-raising careers. Now
he was dating women with fake breasts and grim unwrinkled
smiles. And then there were the women all around us, at the
grocery store, restaurants, the club. We could go on and on
about these young mothers who didn't let their children get a
little tan or climb a little tree or eat a little cotton candy a few
damn times a year when the carnival came to town. And having only one child made it worse. You never learn to relax because you never get a second chance at anything. Every year,
every stage, every phase—it's all new and requires the same
fumbling about. But Tinsley—well, we always had hope for
Tinsley. Were we wrong?

"She's only allowed to have root beer."

"Oh," I said archly, as if that explained it. As if root beer
were somehow more acceptable than a Coca-Cola! As if they
both wouldn't rot your damned teeth! Tinsley was lucky I
didn't give her a few sips of my beer!

There was a long pause, and I've been living on this earth
long enough to understand what that space was supposed to
contain. I gathered up my breath and my pride and filled it.

"Well, I'm sorry, Tinsley, if I did something to upset you
or Ellie."

I heard her sniff on the other end of the line and that
small sound made me cringe. She sounded prissy and particular and whiny in that moment; not the sensible, open-
minded high-energy Tinsley I thought my son had married,
not at all.

"I guess," I sighed, "cancer is a subject one just can't talk
about."

"Oh no, Ann, that's not true. Look, I'm sorry, too. It must

be—well, it must be hard for you. I can't even imagine what you've been through."

I smiled. I had her now, didn't I? At the end of the day, shouldn't a cancer survivor be given the slack to say any damn thing she pleased? A few seconds later the subject was easily changed; we agreed on a time for Ellie's next playdate, and I left for the club, almost guilt free.

After our tennis round, I told Betsy the whole story over a club sandwich and she pointed out how incredibly ironic the whole situation was. Tinsley and Tom sent me their child to learn the family history, but the *medical* history was off-limits! Well, I said, I guess I'd better not mention that my mother had dementia or they'll make me do a Sudoku puzzle before they let me take Ellie out! Betsy tilted her head and said softly that she didn't know dementia ran in my family.

I waved my hand in the air. "One person," I said, "is hardly an epidemic." Well, Betsy rejoined, since you're climbing trees I thought perhaps you'd forgotten how old you are. We laughed and the subject changed to something else.

In the late afternoon I spread the newspaper across my dining room table and laid out scissors, glue, and pipe cleaners in addition to the recently purchased construction paper, poster board, and faux cardinal. Looking at everything laid out that way confounded me. It was like looking at the parts of an engine. I still didn't quite understand what Ellie was going to make of all these pieces, but I'd come to realize it *was* her project, not mine. I was just one of the pieces, like the paper or glue. *Assemble your materials,* her teacher told her. *Lay out your markers, your photos, and your grandmothers.*

When Tom arrived with Ellie, he lingered for a long

time. I invited him twice to stay, but he said he couldn't. Kept asking if we needed supplies, if he could run out and get paper or pipe cleaners.

"No," I said firmly.

"Tinsley has a hot-glue gun if you need it."

I recoiled from the phrase "hot-glue gun" as if I'd been shot.

"No, dear," I said deliberately, "we're all set."

I knew he wanted to say something to me, beyond the discussion I'd had with Tinsley, but he couldn't bring himself to. We'd never had sharp words for each other, Tom and I. Even during the inevitable childhood kerfuffles and adolescent pranks. I couldn't yell at him, and that gave him no reason to yell back. We were wildly unpracticed at arguing with each other. Theo and he could always stir up a heated debate at least, over politics or pending legislation. Not us. Now, he couldn't even summon a stern face.

He finally left, saying he'd be back at nine. Nine, I repeated to myself. *Nine.*

Ellie cut brown construction paper in the shape of a house, then cut smaller houses out of other colors. Her plan, she told me, was to "layer" the houses and decorate the roofline with pipe cleaners. Her name would go on a welcome mat in front of the house, and the bird would be wired into the binding. I nodded. I sensed I shouldn't say anything, but my comments twitched inside me. I blinked, breathed, shifted feet. At one point, when the glue squished out the edges of the third soggy house, I almost had to leave the room, stop watching. She was doing it *wrong*. She was making a mistake, and I was letting her.

"Ellie," I said brightly, "do you think maybe the layers are . . ."

"Too thick?" she said, standing back to survey her progress.

"Yes," I said, relieved.

"Too wet," she added.

"The paper isn't strong enough to support all that glue and pipe cleaners."

She nodded and looked up at me. "Do you have any other ideas?"

I tried to hide my shock. But why was I surprised? Didn't children appreciate their elders only when they were in a pickle?

This vortex was my opportunity, I knew. I had to think quickly. I rubbed my chin with one hand and looked skyward. After a minute something swelled in me, ballooned into being, rising up fuller with each passing second, a feeling familiar from my own classrooms, the old writing desks and dusty labs and lockered hallways of Langley, before it had been renovated and wiped clean of any personality. A brilliant idea forming itself, carving and polishing inside me. I smiled broadly and prepared for its necessary, exuberant birth.

"When exactly is this due?"

"In a week," she said glumly.

"What if . . . ," I said, rising to stand, "we took *new* photos for the cover? To juxtapose with the old?"

When she looked up, her eyes were a tad brighter. I understood what was happening between us. There were words like "juxtapose" that could thrill just with their sound, the music of something bursting forth, clanging itself forward into miraculous change. I wish I could have breathed them over my children's cribs, repeating them instead of singsongs.

"Like . . . what kind of photos?"

"How about," I rubbed my hands together, "I take pictures of you or maybe your mother and father, running, flapping your wings . . ." I paused and moved my own arms slowly, ballerina-like, invoking the grandest of birds. "The camera blurring, showing you in motion? I have a great camera, and I'm not a bad shot. We could take them in black and white to look old."

"Or on the computer," she added brightly, "we could make them that old brown color!"

"Sepia!"

"Yes!"

If we were another sort of pair, we might have cried "Eureka!" or slapped each other high fives. Instead, we set to work. We finished all the interior pages, nestling the photos into plastic sleeves, writing captions. She put all the pieces into the large portfolio envelope she'd brought along, then started cleaning up. She began closing the albums, stacking them. I went to the coat closet to get a hand vacuum for the paper scraps.

"Grandma," she called out, "are there any other family secrets besides the breast cancer?"

My hand went to my heart. I *knew* I hadn't opened the green trunks in the attic. I knew I hadn't brought down the wrong albums. But what had she seen? Could a photo have fallen in and stuck to the back of the album? The birthday photo, the one I kept under my pillow for so long—was that where it had gone?

I turned so quickly I got dizzy. The album in front of her was open to a photo of two boys in letter sweaters swinging my aunt Caro by her legs and arms. I leaned in for a closer look. Caro had her engagement ring on, but my mother did not. Who were these boys? Where was this picture taken?

"Grandma?"

"All families have secrets," I said quietly, with as much tact as I could muster.

"Like what?"

I took a breath; I had to be more careful, I did.

"Oh, it's complicated, sweetheart."

"Too complicated for a kid to understand?"

"Too boring, really," I said and smiled. "Tangled and silly. Not all secrets are interesting, some are just plain silly."

"My mommy has a secret," she said quietly.

"Oh?"

"She has a friend she works out with. Who is a boy."

I swallowed and took a deep breath. Ellie's eyes moved up from the album to meet mine.

"That's different from a boyfriend." She said it as a pronouncement, but I saw the crack in her armor. I felt the fissure coming, as we walked, as if the floor Theo had designed but never built could have opened up at any time.

"Yes, why, yes it is," I said, patting her hand. "Completely different."

"But she told me not to tell anybody." Her voice was soft again and I felt her unease. It was one thing to move closer to your grandmother with a confidence, and another thing to have to move away from your own mother to do it.

I cocked my head. Why would Tinsley do such a thing?

This seemed completely unnecessary, unless . . . was Tom the jealous type? I couldn't recall ever seeing him be overbearing or controlling.

"You know, when you were tiny, she used to take you with her when she ran, in the jogging stroller. She never went anywhere without her little sprout. That's what she called you, 'sprout.'"

I smiled, proud of myself for remembering so clearly. At Tinsley's baby shower her friends had wheeled in that red canvas monstrosity with the enormous tires and everyone oohed and ahhed over it like it was a new car. Tinsley had always liked to be outdoors, baby or no baby. She and Tom were constantly hiking or biking somewhere when they were first married. For their first anniversary, Theo and I had given them a tent, and Tinsley's eyes lit up as if she'd gotten a string of pearls. Tom used to joke that Tinsley was born outside, and found among the leaves, like Mowgli.

"She doesn't take me anymore, and she exercises all the time now," Ellie said quietly and I realized that if you added her statements together, their sum was greater than their parts. Was Tinsley exercising all the time with her friend? Was she worried her husband would be jealous? Was she not spending enough time with her daughter?

"Well," I said, "she probably is just . . . nervous about getting older. Watching her weight, making sure she stays healthy." It seemed to me her fortieth birthday must be approaching. As was Tom's. Maybe instead of having Botox, she was simply working out.

I asked Ellie if she wanted something to drink and she said yes.

I brought out a can of Coca-Cola and two glasses filled with ice.

"To our cover," I said.

Her eyes widened in the glow of the bright red can.

"It can be our tiny secret," I whispered.

We drank deeply, the bubbles tickling our noses. This is how revolutions begin, I wanted to tell her. Just like this.

March 12, 2010

Tinsley and Tom seemed almost too thrilled by our idea for the cover. When they picked Ellie up on Saturday night, and she informed them breathlessly, their faces through the car window took on the animated bluster of clowns. It reminded me of a different kind of photograph, hand tinted, with the sky too bright and everyone's cheeks unnaturally pink. Maybe Tinsley felt guilty because she'd been exercising too much, and was excited to have an opportunity to hover over her daughter one of the evenings she was supposed to be mine.

We met Tuesday evening at Doolittle's Dog Park, near the enormous faux-bois birdbath at the top of the rise. At one time, this was just a park—no dog. It spanned thirty acres and had been annexed off from the main estate and donated by the Forrester family, so everyone could enjoy the rolling meadow view. Now, the township had renamed it after a fictional character and the sign had dog-biscuit artwork painted in the background. I could only hope that the Forresters had once had a dog, and that they weren't howling in their graves.

Tom ran his hand over the birdbath. "Hey, Ellie, we don't have to bathe in it, do we?"

Tinsley laughed loudly, too loudly I thought. She really

had to be careful, with her broad bones and large teeth, of turning horsey as she aged. We all have animals inside, dear.

"No, silly!" Ellie said. "We're going to do other bird things."

"Okay, then, let's go get some twigs, right, Tins?"

"You got it—I'm on twig patrol," she said.

"Huh?" Ellie scrunched up her face.

"Your parents are off to build you a nest."

"Yeah," Tom said, "and then we'll go out to dinner for a big plate of worms!"

"Daddy!"

Tom leaned over to tickle her. The light was thick and yellow as it filtered through the trees, and I didn't want to waste a second of it, so I grabbed some candids of them laughing and joking around. Between giggle fits Ellie tried to explain to her parents what she wanted them to do: to run in circles around the bath, and to flap their arms like birds. Ellie went first, then Tom, then Tinsley. Tom started to squawk and make pterodactyl calls, which made Ellie laugh harder. Everyone's skin glowed and I couldn't help thinking what an exceptionally handsome family they were. Still, smooth skin and handsomeness aside, they weren't moving in a coordinated way, and many of the shots I took were really quite terrible. I started to think I'd been mad to attempt it.

Still, they were having so much fun, who cared? At one point Tinsley flapped her way up to Tom and leaped on his back.

"Help!" he cried. "A hawk has its claws in me!"

He fell to the ground, and on her next lap, Ellie piled onto them and told them to get up and fly. They laughed together and tumbled around, Tinsley's golden and caramel hair flying in all directions, and all my nascent fears about her faded away for a moment.

I took close-ups and wide shots of all their antics, but honestly, no matter what they did, it didn't look like cover material. They just couldn't seem to hit a rhythm; if one was up, the other two were down. Finally I took a nice shot of Tom and Ellie, flapping in unison, but Tinsley was out of synch. I'd never noticed before how oddly long her arms were, so thin in the forearm they appeared in danger of snapping in two.

They kept circling and eventually improved, smoothing their gaits, synching their arms. I just kept pushing the button, not even pausing to look, just hoping I was getting what I was seeing, and more. Those little in-between moments when people forget they are posing, and just keep moving. Thank god I'd left the Nikon at home and brought my little digital camera—I would have wasted roll after roll of film.

"I have an idea!" Ellie said suddenly, breathlessly, before she stopped and ran to the birdbath. She proceeded to climb onto the rim while her mother kept telling her to be careful. She flapped on the edge, as if she was about to leap, and I thought, that's it, that's the cover. Just her. Not the others. Her. I took a dozen shots, each better than the last.

The next day when I picked up my prints at what used to be the butcher shop and was now Staples, the young man who waited on me must have seen it, too. Because as he totaled up my purchase he said he would be happy to go in and do any cropping or enlarging I wanted for a dollar fifty per print. That didn't strike me as something he said to every customer, like the admonition to supersize. He'd seen something and was offering an improvement: *crop out that older couple next to the kid and you'll really have something awesome there.*

After I finished and had the prints in my car, I drove around for a long time before I delivered them to Ellie. I told myself I was just touring the old haunts, seeing what was new, what the developers were up to. I was just doing a neighborly reconnaissance, keeping an eye on what new restaurant had taken over the little tailor shop, and whether the bank had succumbed to evening hours. I stopped in front of Luddington Park, thinking I might take a stroll, but the human traffic looked a bit thick to merge into. I watched the joggers panting and huffing, and the bicyclers spinning and leaning, all along a thin winding path that was only ever meant to hold a mother, a baby, and a lightweight collapsible stroller. I sighed and tried to think of somewhere to go next, and couldn't come up with a damn thing. When I was married to Theo and felt trapped in the house, I used to go to the train station and pretend to be waiting for someone. At the first sound of the whistle, I'd arrange my face expectantly, scan the crowd for a familiar pair of eyes, then sigh and look at my watch. It gave me something to do, that little piece of playacting. It gave me a small purpose.

Now, it wasn't that I felt trapped so much; I just wanted to freeze the moment in time. I didn't want to go to her house with those photographs; I wanted to take the prints and hide them, lose them, start over again. All Ellie had to do was glue in her essay, and bind the pages with raffia. The project had ended. What now?

I'd hoped the Generations reception at the Langley School would be festive. I imagined a bowl of punch and trays of little cakes, and pictured some sort of slide show or video presentation, with our cover sparkling and Ellie's name in lights. Perhaps there would be some sort of competition, with a blue ribbon presented to her by the principal in the middle of a well-lit stage. Ellie had worked so hard. Surely my alma mater would recognize these efforts with appropriate fanfare. I realized later I was picturing an event similar to my high school reunion. Silly me.

I arrived in the middle of an overlit gymnasium filled with people eating crumbly muffins and holding cups of lukewarm coffee. As I walked amid the sea of mounted covers and projects, I smelled not the thrillingly creative aroma of glue or paint or Magic Markers, but the scent of dirty rubber sneakers. I imagine if you ran a hand over any surface in the gym you would not find dust, but the ground-down detritus of black waffle-bottom shoes.

We entered together, Ellie, Tom, Tinsley, and I, and soon split up. Tinsley and Tom joined the other parents they knew, who stood in small circles between weighted balloons at the edges of the new gymnasium, while Ellie and I joined the other children leading their grandparents through the maze of projects. When I attended Langley, back in the day, this patch of land was a softball field; now it held this domed and overly lit bubble that was supposed to inspire play. I still remember the old structure on the other side of the school's entrance, more barn than gymnasium. You couldn't serve a volleyball without brushing your fist against the wooden wall. Peter's prep school was across the way, and he'd walk over after chess club and watch us play. I couldn't hear him cheering through the window, but I'd see him, fists pumped in the air, whenever I scored a point. That old gym was almost unrecognizable now; they'd bathed it with windows and called it a greenhouse.

The winding trail of grandparents lingered over every child's project, sniping and comparing, while their grandchild pulled on their hand, anxious to get to *theirs*. Ellie and I were no exception.

"No one else has a new photo on the cover," I noted somewhat gleefully. "Everyone else has old photos."

We passed by an acre of xeroxed black-and-white portraits of couples, some lumpy and foreboding, some lipsticked and smiling. How alike all these projects looked, as if the children had furtively copied from each other during study hall. And I couldn't help noticing four other projects cut out in the shape of something—what a merciful accident we'd had, with those failed layers of paper and glue!

When we reached Ellie's display, several other grandmothers and children stood in front of it.

"It's awfully new looking," one of the grandmothers

whispered. She herself was old looking, with a teased globe of hair and fat, sensible shoes.

At the next display the same grandmother whispered, "I don't think a child drew that picture, do you? Who is her grandpa, Andrew Wyeth?"

"You should be very proud, Ellie," I whispered. "It's the best one here."

"I know," she whispered back with a huge sigh and squeezed my hand. There were no drips of glue, or uneven edges, the signs of haste. We'd taken our time, and it showed.

To celebrate, we went out for dinner to a place where the smell of a wood-fired pizza oven permeated the entire room. I coughed when I walked in; it was a bit like being in a hut where they were about to roast a goat.

"This has always been Ellie's favorite restaurant," Tinsley said.

"Really?" I choked out.

Instead of crayons, they gave the children dough to play with. Tinsley reassured me that there was no raw egg in it. "They pasteurize it first," she said and smiled, as if that made a difference, as if I cared, as if I hadn't eaten enough cookie and pie dough to kill me ten times over.

"Oh, how lovely," I said.

"Ann," she said, fiddling with the rustic napkin on her lap, "have you ever made cookies when Ellie was over and eaten the dough?"

I blinked at my daughter-in-law.

"No, we usually pick wild mushrooms in the backyard and sauté them," I replied, and Tom, god bless him, laughed.

"An old family tradition," he added. "Remember when we found the wild onions, Mom? I told you the daffodils smelled funny."

"Yes, yes, I believe we made soup from them."

"You made soup from something you found in the yard?" Tinsley said.

Tom and I stared at her as if she'd lost her marbles.

"People generally have their vegetable gardens in their yards," Tom said.

"That's not the same thing, honey," she replied.

Tinsley gestured to our waiter and Tom glanced over at me with a rueful smile. I widened my eyes back at him, but said nothing. It wouldn't do to gang up on Tinsley in front of Ellie; no sense in blurting out, "You're insane, it is the same thing!"

When the waiter came over, Tinsley asked for sparkling water, and said that Ellie could have a Sprite if she wanted. Ellie smiled but gave me a sideways glance. I knew what she really wanted: Coca-Cola. Tom and I each ordered a glass of merlot, and the waiter wondered if we'd like a bottle for the table. We looked at each other and Tom squinted, considering.

"Oh, I only want one glass," I said, and I swear I could hear Tinsley exhale. She was watching me, I knew. Not looking at me, watching.

The drinks arrived and Tinsley raised her glass.

"To our darling Ellie," Tinsley said. "To a job well done!"

We all clinked glasses and drank and Tinsley asked Ellie if, as the guest of honor, she'd like to make a speech.

"Yes," Ellie said, standing up and lifting her glass again. "To Grandma! For helping me."

"Thank you, sweetheart, but you did all the work. All I did was bring out the albums," I said.

"And the snacks," she added, and we all laughed.

"I'm sure," Tinsley said and smiled, "Ann did a lot more than that."

Ellie started rolling her dough into a long coiled snake as Tom spoke about his firm's newest client, a pharmaceutical company accused of using tainted vaccine. He said he was glad he hadn't been asked to defend them, since one of their friends had an autistic child and claimed the vaccine had been the cause.

"Can't you turn down assignments, now that you're a partner?" I asked.

He shrugged, and I saw Ellie in him then, the not giving anything away.

"If you'd lived through the polio epidemic, you'd understand how important vaccines are," I added.

"It's probably not the best dinner conversation with a little one, though, Tom," Tinsley said.

"What?" Ellie said, looking up from the small snake eyes she'd just formed.

"Nothing, honey," Tom replied. "Just grown-up talk about diseases and stuff."

"If I'm going to be a doctor, I need to know about what you're talking about."

"Do you want to be a doctor, baby?"

"Maybe," she said. "Then I could cure Grandma's breast cancer."

I dropped my head to avoid Tinsley's gaze, but couldn't help allowing a smile to curl up on the edges of my mouth.

I had inspired her! This is what they write about in people's autobiographies, the exact moment their passions took hold!

"Sweetie," Tinsley said softly, "Grandma isn't sick anymore."

"I meant cure it for everyone."

Tinsley blinked. "Oh."

"Ellie," I said, emboldened, turning to her in the half-circle booth, "doing this project together gave me an idea. What if," I said, my eyes dancing, "you and I had a regular get-together to do crafts?"

"Like a playdate?" Her eyes seemed to brighten.

"Yes, just like that. We could do it perhaps twice a month, or once a month if you're busy."

"Great idea," Tom said, but Tinsley was quiet, and so was Ellie for just a moment. She glanced at her mother nervously before she looked back at me. Had I read her wrong? Had they discussed something I wasn't privy to? I thought if I asked them in a group, in public, they couldn't say no. The same way Tom used to ask if his friend could stay for dinner when the child was standing right in front of me with a rumbling stomach.

Ellie's brief silence—two seconds? three?—crushed me in the way that only a child can crush you. I felt my face start to flush on the edges.

"*I* think that would be fun," she said with a nod of her head for punctuation.

"We have to look at your schedule, though," Tinsley said, frowning. "And see if you even have a couple of hours free."

Ellie didn't look at her mother, but she flashed me a small conspiratorial smile.

I smiled back widely. "Yes, of course, Tinsley," I said brightly, "and I'll look at mine."

When the pasta dishes arrived, the plates were enormous and steaming in a way that struck me as false, like a restaurant commercial. I could have eaten for a week off my plate of primavera alone. I thought of our visit to Stuart's, and the genius of those old red plastic baskets: they always held a perfectly sized portion.

When we finished eating Tom slipped his arm around his wife and she squirmed a little beneath his grasp. If I had just been looking, I wouldn't have noticed, but I was watching. Oh, I was watching her now, too.

July 1, 1967

shallow bath

THE BABY HAS BEEN SITTING up for weeks, but he didn't smile properly until today when I got back from the doctor, after Betsy put him down for his nap. He was in his crib, kicking that excited, jerky baby kick that looks like it hurts to do, and when I leaned over to pick him up, he smiled from ear to ear.

"What are you smiling for?" I asked with a sigh. "Huh? What are you so happy about? This is not a happy day, silly."

My breast had been hurting more than usual, so Dr. Ferrell's office fit me in right away. The nurse said it was probably a clogged milk duct, and I nodded my agreement as she handed me a gown. Of course that was what it was, what else could it be?

Dr. Ferrell's hands seemed colder than usual as he fingered each breast, his eyes focused on a painting of a seascape over my head. I told him it was on the left side and when his fingers pressed there, I winced.

"Hmmm," he said.

"What does that mean?"

"Well, Ann, there's an irregularity here. Could be nothing, but we'll have to be sure."

"And if it's not nothing?"

"It could be a benign growth. Or . . . it could be a cancer-ous growth."

"My mother had breast cancer," I said quietly.

"Yes, sometimes there's a correlation, but not always. Let's not be hasty."

I nodded, and he told me he needed to do a biopsy, but as he called in the nurse and laid out the tools on the tray, he neglected to tell me that it would hurt like hell. That it would feel like I was being excavated, drilled for oil. Drilled for cancer.

When I'd called Theo to tell him, the first question he'd asked was, "Which one." Which one! As if he had a favorite breast; as if he was rooting for one over the other, army vs. navy. Imagine uttering that after hearing the word "biopsy." I suppose he was so distracted with his damned new shopping mall he didn't remember all the times I'd complained about the right one being sore. He forgot, the same way I forget which client he's meeting with, who is building the shopping court as opposed to the corporate plaza.

When he is in the office, he doesn't think about the mess at home, just as I don't think about the war and all the bodies in Vietnam unless I turn on the television.

Really, Theo, I'd replied, what does it matter which one? And he said he wondered if it was the same one that had been sore, or the other one. Well. At least there was a rea-sonable explanation. At least he'd remembered something. But as always, I wanted more. I wanted him to feel bad that he hadn't come to the appointment with me. I wanted him to read my mind. I wanted him to come home. I told him the test would be back in a week, and he asked what the prognosis was, and I told him it was either cancer or it wasn't. In a week, I said, I'll either have one breast or two. And he swallowed hard—I could hear it through the phone—and said we'd cross that bridge when we came to it. Yes, I said. I don't want you to worry until you need to worry, he said.

The baby cooed, as if sensing my mind had wandered away, and I smiled back, out of some kind of automatic, electric obligation, and we stood there together, all gums and teeth, pink and white and gleaming. And for a moment, the same moment, all the world would have believed we were both happy. Is that all good mothering is? Synchronicity?

I carried him over to the window to look out at the sun peeking over Luddington Park. Just a few months before, we'd petitioned to save it, Betsy and I and the other mothers in the neighborhood. We fought the rezoning for office space, and we won when it turned out the mayor's wife had always loved it, had played leapfrog there as a child. There was talk of naming it after her: Elinor Park. Betsy and I laughed at this idea, threatened to carve our own names in the sign. General Luddington was a decorated war hero; Elinor Parker was a college dropout who married a civil servant.

I pointed out the window and the baby's face turned serious again, studious, as if he felt our struggle over the land. His face looked as if I were his teacher, not his mother, and the moment was gone. Sun turned to cloud. He grabbed a lock of my hair and I held his bouncing fist, trying to keep it away from the bandage and the stitches underneath.

I suppose the baby's lack of smiling is my fault for not cajoling him more, not tickling him enough or sweet-talking him like a pet. I always think I don't have the time, but the truth is, I haven't the energy. Haven't felt up to cooing over anyone or anything, not since he was born. I was like this with Emma, too, I remember. Just do what needs to be done. Just get through the day and try to get some sleep. I've never had those warm feelings running through me like syrup, the way other women do; I have to conjure them up.

And Theo—he's like a third child waiting patiently until I'm done with the others, waiting to ask me for what he needs. Could I look at his new drawings? Could he invite the Lehmans over for fondue? Could I recommend a hairdresser for his new client's wife, the one with the Jackie Kennedy bob who just moved here from Memphis? And the way he looked at his dinner plate last night—staring at the cheese-and-asparagus omelet as if it had landed from a flying saucer.

"It's your favorite omelet." I said it so brightly the syllables bounced like springs.

"Yes, it is, how novel."

"It's hardly novel, Theo, when you've eaten it for years."

"How novel to have it for dinner, I mean."

He smiled at me, but I didn't smile back. The baby will learn eventually: it doesn't always work.

I ate my eggs in large bites, the same way Theo had eaten skirt steak the night before, and lamb chops the night before that. I wanted to scream that even Julia Child said it wasn't easy to make a perfect omelet, that he was lucky he had warm food—Betsy had made liverwurst and pickle sandwiches for her family last week! He ate a few bites, politely, then pushed away from the table. When he stood up, the scoot of his antique chair sounded like kindling snapping.

I sat there trying to remember the last time someone had rejected something I had made with my own two hands, and the only person I could name was Emma, and she was a child. Even the misshapen cupcakes and slightly burned cookies I'd made in high school for the Langley bake sale had been greedily gobbled up by Peter and his friends.

Theo had always been particular; it was a trait architects were prone to, if you listened to the other wives at his firm. When we first started dating, I found it charming: he'd always arrive in a freshly washed car, and when we walked into a restaurant, he'd never settle for an ill-placed table. One time he came to my mother's carriage house with steel wool and a tin of green stain, and repainted her peeling wooden mailbox for her. I thought this was a sign that he'd be good around the house, that he'd do what needed to be done.

The true surprise of the last few years is how different he is as a parent than a husband. He may do what's asked, but doesn't think of anything on his own, like an unmotivated employee. Surely he could not have always been that way. Betsy once said his eyes were so beautiful, his gaze was like a gift. Did Theo know this, too? That if push came to shove, he could just look at someone instead of doing or saying the right thing? Was that how he enchanted his clients, by warming them with the fire of his eyes?

It seemed the closer Theo moved toward opening that

shopping mall, the later he worked, the more he focused on his own needs, the light in his eyes seemed further and further away. I wonder if, instead of being a couple who grows closer, knowing each other more intimately, we are going in reverse, on our way back to being strangers again.

July 8, 1967

THEY WERE SUPPOSED TO CALL with the biopsy results today, but didn't.

In the afternoon, to pass the time more than anything else, I popped popcorn for Emma, and she seemed fascinated with the process, how I moved the pan across the stove, how the kernels sprang to life with a metallic ping. A little too fascinated, I thought. I'd have to be careful she wasn't left alone with the stove; she was just the kind of child who would turn it on when you weren't looking. In the afternoon, when I kissed her before her nap, her chin and cheeks were still buttery. It reminded me of that first high school baseball game with Peter, when we shared a tub of popcorn and he kissed me at the short end of the bleachers. Our lips were slick, and traces of salt lingered at the corners of his mouth. Ah, the things you remember. Little things. Sweet things.

I went into the drawer with my hose and bras and burrowed around, digging up my journal from last year, looking to see what I'd written about Peter after our high school reunion. Just wanting to remember, to savor a few details. But when I turned to May, there was no entry that day. I didn't write every day, just on the particularly bad or particularly good days, it seemed. I thought I'd written something about the reunion, though. A discreet little something, surely. I'd come home so energized, inspired and alive, not even feeling the numbing of the glasses of punch. The next morning, however, I had that unique combination of headache and regret. Is that why I neglected to write a note about it?

When I went upstairs to put the journal back, it suddenly bothered me that my books were all in different places. The old ones in the attic, last years' in the hose drawer, the current one in a stack on my bedside table. I took last year's and put it in the trunk in the attic. I could imagine opening it years later, and having my secret float up to me: carrying the guilt, but also the beauty, of what can happen when two people come together at exactly the wrong time.

But no, apparently I didn't tell anyone; not my diary, not Betsy, not Aunt Caro, not even my mother, who was the safest person of all to tell, because she, god bless her, would forget it the very next day.

March 30, 2010

I took stock of Tinsley's gratitude warily, suspicious of it in the way another person might have suspected silence. She had always been a happy sort of person, almost twinkly when she had a glass or two of wine at Christmas. I remember one occasion, early on, surrounded by bigwigs at the opening of one of Theo's shopping centers, when she was so ebullient over Theo having wooden benches mounted outside the stores—*What a smart idea! What lovely, sturdy materials!*—that Tom and I practically rolled our eyes. But now, with no holiday in sight, no celebration or cameras, and no alcohol on her breath, she was just too effusive. Every other time Ellie and I had gotten together she seemed a bit nervous and wary, worried about where I would drive her and what I would feed her. But now, taking me up on my offer to take Ellie for a walk and out to lunch so Tinsley could exercise or play squash this morning, she stood on my porch and told me how *thoughtful* I was, and how *difficult* it was to fit in her "workouts" on the weekends, and that Tom worked so much he couldn't offer much support, but it meant a lot to her to have her mother-in-law to lean on. Blah blah blah.

Of course, it *was* morning, and a person had to allow for

the overindulgence of coffee these days. Maybe that's why she was running off at the mouth. Maybe that's why her face was red. That, or she was uncomfortable for some reason—as if she were hiding something and attempting to cover it up with a pile of nouns and verbs.

Of course, I hadn't told her the truth, either; that this was my mother's birthday, and that I thought, to honor her, Ellie and I might talk more about her, and look at more of her things.

Ellie was wearing a sweat suit that at first glance appeared to be made of navy velvet, and which I prayed was merely velour. I am not in favor of this style of dressing, my belief being that a polo shirt, cardigan, and proper-fitting trousers were just as comfortable and eminently better suited to most nongymnastic activities.

"Are you having a 'workout,' too?" I kidded her, and she just looked at me, shaking her head. She was so young, she didn't even understand that sweat suits were designed for sweating, not for riding on airplanes or having "playdates" with your grandmother.

"She likes to be comfortable when she's not wearing her school uniform," Tinsley said.

"Don't we all," I replied.

"We'll see you around two, then?"

I nodded and Tinsley leaned over to tousle her daughter's hair. Ellie frowned and ducked away and the movement stung with memory; I felt a pain, literally, in the rib near my heart.

"Kiss your mother good-bye, Ellie," I said firmly.

Tinsley's eyes met mine over Ellie's head, and there it

was, that gratitude again. We've all juggled children and households and traveling husbands, I wanted to say. You're not alone, my dear. But I didn't. She smiled at us and then she was gone, practically bouncing down my porch steps with sheer joy.

I'd taken a long bath early this morning, well before Ellie was due to come over, and had my hair blown dry at the Hair Cottage. Since Ellie had been just the slightest bit reluctant to set up our playdate, the last thing I wanted to do was embarrass her with a grandma who looked frumpy or smelled a bit off.

Now she was with me in the dining room, nibbling on a cookie, and I nibbled one, too, just to keep her company, to have an excuse to be near her. I leaned over, breathing her in. She smelled of strawberries and milk. It was a smell you wanted in your life forever, like laundry on the line, or the dusty ears of a well-loved teddy bear. I imagined it was the smell of fresh shampoo. I liked to think she'd taken measures, too.

When she finished her second cookie she looked up expectantly, with a "now what shall we do?" look on her face that indicated she had no real ideas of her own. I was beginning to see a trend; I could ride this trend, yes.

"I thought," I began, "that in a little while, it might be fun to go out and take some photographs together, then go have lunch."

"Photographs of what?"

"Oh, I don't know, whatever we find. There's a squirrel's nest in the park where they swing from the trees like chimpanzees."

She shrugged, which was better than lodging an objection. She paused then said, "You said in a little while. What about now?"

"Now," I leaned in conspiratorially, "I thought I'd show you another family secret. Like you asked about." I picked up a flashlight I'd laid on the sideboard.

"Really?" she said, eyes wide.

"You see, today is my mother's birthday, and one of the secrets is about her."

She followed me to the attic stairs and when I pulled them down, a puff of dust came with them. I told her to go up first but she hesitated, so I said she could follow me. I turned on the flashlight and we walked up. I headed straight to the dark brown trunks. I had nestled the small safe in one of them earlier in the day, for dramatic effect.

"This," I said, kneeling down with some effort, "is where the photo albums were."

I opened one of the trunks and pulled out the safe. "And this," I said with a flourish, "is almost all that's left of my mother's fortune." I dialed the combination, aware that the metallic spin mesmerized her. I pulled out the ring box and held it aloft. Her eyes were wide and I nodded my permission.

As she opened the box, I held the flashlight above her so the gem would sparkle. Her mouth dropped open.

"Did you used to be rich?"

"Yes. My mother came from a very wealthy family. They owned a lot of railroad land, and a lot of land in general. When I was growing up we had three houses in different cities and servants in each one."

"Wow, Grandma, that's cool."

"It was, rather. Until my father started stealing from my mother, liquidating stock portfolios and hiding money in offshore accounts. That was not so *cool*."

"Did he go to jail?" Ellie whispered.

"No, my mother didn't know what was going on at first. And my father was so nimble, nothing could be proved."

I told her that when my father left he said he was going on an extended trip, doing business in Hong Kong; the day he left I went shopping for a prom gown, oblivious. When I came home I rushed into the living room to show my mother, tearing open the box from Bryant's Department Store, exclaiming over the turquoise satin, too giddy over my purchase to take notice of my mother's detached distance. She told me the dress was beautiful and that she had to go down to the bank, that there was a "glitch" with one of their accounts. That's the word she used, "glitch." She came back from the meeting dumbfounded and dizzy, but said it was nothing, she just had a little headache. She kept the truth from me for over a month, and it was only when June arrived, and it was time to go to Nantucket, that she broke the news: while I had gone to my graduation parties and prom, she had sold her family's cabin in the Adirondacks, and both her Nantucket homes, even the cottage, to pay for taxes. In less than a year's time, she would sell our main house and move into a cottage on Aunt Caro's estate. She'd managed to hide only the emerald when she got wind of what was going on.

"How old were you?" Ellie asked.

"Nearly seventeen."

"Did he take anything from you?"

"Well, I just explained, Ellie, that—"

"Did he take your clothes or your toys?"

"Well, no, but he took away my inheritance, my family home, my summerhouse and summer plans, everything."

"So you couldn't go to college?"

"Well, no, he made provisions to pay for that. But that's all."

"Oh," she nodded. "What about when he died?"

"He left me seventy-five thousand dollars. The rest went to his new wife."

"Isn't that a lot of money, though?"

I sighed. "It covered your father's schooling."

She nodded.

"Don't you start taking his side now, little one, just because he made me a bird house once."

"I didn't say anything, Grandma."

"All right then. It's my mother's birthday, remember. We must take her side."

There was no pity in her eyes. Was college all a person should expect from a parent? I remember my college graduation, how I surveyed the crowd like a Secret Service agent, scanning the faces for his. Not wanting to see him, not wanting to miss him. And later, how he waited until my mother and Aunt Caro had gone. I can still picture the outline of his sheepish frame as he lumbered up to me and my friends. The way he shook their hands solemnly as their wide eyes questioned me over his shoulder, wondering why I'd never mentioned that I'd even *had* a father. I'd pretended, as I recall, that he was dead.

"Annie," he said. "I know you don't understand this, not yet, but I did what I had to do. What was fair to do."

"Fair, Dad? Are you crazy?"

"I made sure you got to college, at least, even after I—"

"Even after what, Daddy? After you decided to hate me because I had the bad luck of looking like her?"

"It's complicated, Ann-o," he said softly.

The ring box remained in Ellie's curled palm. "Hey, are you okay, Grandma?"

I waved my memories out of the air like a bad odor. "Of course I am."

"It's a sad story. You must have missed your daddy after he left."

I swallowed hard. "Well, I was older, it wasn't as if I were truly a child anymore."

"But you only have one father," she said.

"Yes," I said softly. "Well, would you like to try the ring on?"

"Oh yes!" She twirled it on her index finger. "My mommy hides things from Daddy, too."

I swallowed hard before I dared to answer.

"Really?" I smoothed the fabric in the trunk, trying to be nonchalant.

She nodded. "When she buys shoes she always says, 'Don't tell Daddy.'"

"Oh," I said quietly. Did the disappointment seep into my voice?

She twirled the ring on her hand. "This looks just like the one in the photo."

"What's that?"

Ellie was silent, reverential, as she looked at the ring with her head cocked.

"There was a ring like this in one of the photos."

"Oh, I doubt it, dear. My aunt said my mother never wore it."

"No, I think she did. My mom showed it to me."

"Tinsley? When on earth—"

"When I took home the albums that day, Daddy said, 'That's my grandma,' and my mom said it was a really pretty ring and wondered whether you had it."

"I see," I sniffed. Trolling for jewelry before I was even sick, let alone dead? Tinsley had to be more careful now—I had a spy!

"Well, sometime when we don't have luncheon plans, perhaps we can find the photo."

She nodded and followed me to the stairs. "What's in those?" she asked innocently, pointing to the two green trunks in the corner.

"Oh, nothing. Baby things," I said dismissively, with a wave of my hand. I couldn't bear to glance at them, but she did, lingering in front of them after I was already on the stairs. I reached back for her hand to tug her along and she let me hold it for a few moments before she pulled away.

Downstairs I poured us each a glass of cola and I raised mine to hers.

"Well, to my dear mother on her birthday," I said.

"To my great-grandmother," she replied, and the sound of that phrase nearly broke my heart.

My plan was to walk into Bryn Mawr Village, since it

was sunny outside, and quite pleasant for the end of March. We weren't even two blocks into the walk before Ellie fell behind my brisk pace.

"Grandma, if I get tired, will you give me a piggyback ride?"

"Absolutely not."

"Oh."

"If you get tired, we'll lie down in the hedges and nap with the hedgehogs!" I said and she giggled so loud it was a squeal. It hung in the air like a bell, like something you could see.

I crossed the street, and she followed me, skipping. We followed Barrett Lane until it turned onto the curving walkway that looped around the college. On clear days like this one, the path pulsed with students and the buzz of music coming from their earphones. Some walked, but most jogged, alone or in packs of ten or twenty in some semblance of uniform. Track teams, soccer teams. Even older people seemed influenced by the rhythms of the college, and joined them on the path. Everyone was in training for something. The energy around us seemed to feed Ellie, and for a long time she was able to keep up with me. The camera swung around my neck, but the tree where I'd seen the squirrels leaping the day before was empty, and I didn't see anything else worthy enough to document.

It was still early, and not nearly as crowded as it would be at 2 or 3:00, so we were able to walk side by side without having to avoid anyone. A few college girls passed us, with bouncing ponytails and springy sneakers that made them look like they could catapult moonward.

"Promise me you'll never wear a verb or a noun on your bottom."

"I promise, Grandma," she said, and I buzzed with pride when she called me that.

Another jogger zoomed around us, so close we had to dodge her droplets of sweat. So close the words on her yellow pants were abundantly clear: CHIQUITA.

Bryn Mawr Diner wasn't really in Bryn Mawr proper. If it was, it would be on the edge of Bryn Mawr College's campus instead of the edge of Villanova's. Its green neon OPEN sign was almost as large as the small building; as we approached you could hear its thrum against the windowpanes. There was a short line for tables, but Stuart's was too far away to be practical, so I pointed Ellie toward the counter. I ordered a club sandwich and Ellie decided on pancakes. She looked up at me as she poured the river of syrup, as if waiting for an admonition that never came. What, I'd like to know, is the point of eating pancakes without at least a decent-size tributary of syrup? When she offered me a bite I poured even more syrup on it, and she smiled.

Afterward we wandered through the small downtown. Over the years it had become more and more oriented to the college—vintage clothing, used books and music stores, a "raw foods" restaurant where all the patrons looked pale. At the art store I bought Ellie a new set of markers for her next project. Outside the thrift shop, a pair of young men played guitar and when they saw Ellie, segued into "Thank Heaven for Little Girls." It was a cheap trick but it worked—I gave her a quarter to toss into their case, and she insisted I take a picture of them, as if they were famous. She stood at the edge of the frame, smiling.

Halfway home, the sun directly in our eyes, Ellie's energy started to flag. She walked so slowly I heard her sneakers scraping on the sidewalk, and I had to keep turning around to make sure she was there. I motioned toward a bus shelter on the opposite edge of campus, and even though we were almost home, suggested we take a break.

I've tried hard to remember every detail of sitting there—how long we lingered, who else walked by first, the faces and gaits of the knot of joggers who swallowed Tinsley and her friend before and after we saw them, as if they were a Secret Service detail designed to keep them out of sight.

I saw her first, not him. It was the familiar flash of light in her hair that caught my eye, which I'd seen so many times in the sunshine of an Easter egg hunt, or the twinkle of a Christmas tree. Lots of women have streaked hair but Tinsley's highlights had a particular golden glint, flying loose around her head like maypole ribbons, and I saw them right away. Her hair, then her, then him.

"Look, it's your mother," bubbled out of my mouth, regrettably, as soon as I saw the hair. Ellie stood up and looked in the same direction, not speaking, the way children do when they're truly concentrating. I stood up, too, but I don't know why. To protect her? To leap in front of the view?

"Take a picture of her, Grandma," Ellie said excitedly and I raised the camera to my eye too quickly, finding my focus too easily. Tinsley's companion came into the frame through my viewfinder, and he looked wrong, all wrong, like

a tourist wandering onto a film set. Their elbows bumped and
my finger snapped the photo quickly, as if I could capture her
before he did. Then, in close up, in miniature, his arm looped
around her as they ran in synch, and he kissed her, lingering
there, though it must have been difficult, coordinating feet,
arm, mouth. Did I admire their grace, the duet of effort? Was
it a beautiful image, the light just right on her buttery hair? Is
that why my finger clicked again just before he pulled away?
Why, I can't precisely say.

We stayed where we were. The Plexiglas enclosure of the
bus shelter was cracked on both sides. It reminded me of cups
that had gone through the dishwasher, and survived, intact,
but not the same.

"Did he just kiss my mom?" Ellie looked at me with a
deep furrow in her brow, a portent of her older, angrier self.

Here it was, I thought. The rightness I sought, my hunch
realized, and I didn't want it anymore, wanted only what we
had before. I still tasted butter and syrup at the edges of my
mouth, the smeared napkin, diner coffee, the cheap sweetness
I longed to have last.

"Just a good-bye kiss. Lots of grown-ups do that," I replied. I wasn't lying to her. I was stating a fact.

"They weren't on a doorstep," she said quietly. "Or near
a car."

"The path splits," I said. "He probably lives off to the
left." I lifted my hand, fluttering it in that direction. Tinsley's
house was straight ahead, not far, perhaps half a mile. They
were out of sight now, over the last small rise, and could be
anywhere. Together, or not.

We walked back slowly and didn't talk much. The camera hung around my neck like a heavy stone, pulling. We stopped at a pond next to the local McDonald's, where some toddlers were feeding French fries to the geese, straight out of their hands, squealing at the threat of being nipped.

"Fries probably aren't good for geese," Ellie said quietly, throwing a pebble into the water.

"Nonsense," I replied. "Birds eat all kinds of things. In New York City, the pigeons prefer hot dogs to birdseed."

On another day, there would have been questions, perhaps. What did birds eat in Philadelphia? Do geese eat differently from pigeons? But not today. We had only a few blocks left to walk, and I felt bad that I couldn't carry her. It was as if she'd known she might need a piggyback ride.

The block where she lived was quiet. The houses were close enough that you could hear a door slam or a vase break, but there was nothing to listen to. Outside her front door, Ellie thanked me, as if she didn't expect me to come inside. But I opened the door and followed her in. In the back of the house, Tinsley stood at the small kitchen island, looking through the mail, her face flushed, her hair caught up in a bun. The golden pieces in front looked wavy now, dull and damp from all her effort.

She didn't hear us.

Ellie took her markers up to her room and I cleared my throat.

Tinsley looked up with a start; I forced a smile.

"She's just run upstairs," I said. "We had a fine time."

"Oh, okay. Thanks so much, Ann," she said, her wrists poised above the mail as one might be above a meal, anxious to get back to it.

When I got home I forced myself to look at the pictures. There was less in them than I remembered, no telling smile of contentment or blush of shame. What struck me most was the shape of his hand on her cheek, the stoutness of his thick fingers, the width of his palm's shadow, so different from my own son's delicate hands.

August 2, 1967

3:00 PM

sponge bath

MY BREAST IS GONE, BUT sometimes I still feel it. When the left one fizzes with milk, I feel the right one, too. When I take off my bra, an imagined weight pulls on both sides. Then I look down, and I know. Betsy and I had a laugh over this—that now I really never could burn my bra even if I wanted to.

This morning I stood in front of the open bathroom window, letting my hair dry in the breeze. I felt it curl up only at the ends; it would never be stick straight like Faye Dunaway's or Jane Fonda's, just as it would never be wavy like Grace Kelly's. I will never be in style, but that is probably the least of my worries. When I lifted my arms, the breeze gathered force across the bandages on my right side, like wind picking up momentum in an alley. Will I ever get used to it? Will I always notice every little thing?

When Dr. Ferrell had called with the biopsy results, I knew what he was going to say. "It's cancer, isn't it?" I said quietly, watching as the bacon I'd just turned popped and sizzled in the cast-iron pan. He said yes, and that he was sorry. He didn't ask how I knew; maybe he assumed my fate was sealed because of my mother. He suggested a date for the surgery and advised me to wean the baby completely beforehand. But I still had a little milk. This morning I crept into the nursery and cradled the baby until his mouth opened and started to burrow, even sleeping, even blind. I opened my shirt and guided him on. I cupped his feet with my right hand to keep him from kicking against my dressing, and closed my eyes. In a few minutes my breast was flat, the skin almost papery. He cried loudly when I pulled him off, cried as I burped him, cried in his crib while I went downstairs to get him a bottle, my shirt still unbuttoned. My son, it seems, would miss my right breast more than anyone else. Was that what I wanted? To know someone would?

Theo brought me home from the hospital and propped pillows all around me, as if to compensate, somehow, for my own new lack of padding. He made a point of looking me straight in the eye, whenever he spoke, trying to train his eyes to not look at my body. I tell you this so you'll know he was trying. He stayed home from the office, working in the study, on that first day, and when it became clear I would need help beyond that, hired a nurse for a week to feed and diaper the baby, make Emma supper and give her a bath. What else could he do? My family couldn't help—my mother was half mad in the nursing home, and Aunt Caro was traveling overseas. It was both thoughtful and necessary to have another person there, but I became dangerously accustomed to it. The day after the nurse left, I clanged around the kitchen angrily, furious at lids that didn't fit pots, at the vague smears of butter and jelly Theo had left on his breakfast plate. The baby was still sleeping but I'd woken up Emma.

"Stop it!"

She called from behind me and I sighed as I whisked the eggs. Who spoke in this rough way? Where had she soaked it up—at the nursery school I paid for? At the playground I'd fought so hard to keep in her life?

"What did you say?"

"I can't sleep," she pouted as she covered her ears with her hands. "That baby always cries and you're making noise."

There was a moment when her voice turned into Theo's. Throaty and ugly, a man in her mouth. Was that who Emma was, Theo's darkest thoughts and deeds embodied? I imagined he felt exactly the same way and was so polite he didn't dare speak of it. I breathed deeply and kept my voice calm.

"You're not supposed to sleep, Emma," I sighed. "It's morning."

I poured orange juice into her favorite plastic cup, an orange bottom with a yellow lid, and handed it to her before I went back to scrambling eggs. When I turned around, she picked it up and I swear she brought it up to her lips, a centimeter away, which is why I didn't see it coming.

The cup could have hit anywhere else and hurt less. Her aim was true, almost straight to the heart: direct to the right breast. I shrieked and collapsed; it hurt so much, so instantaneously, I gagged, nearly vomiting on my own feet.

Emma's hands covered her mouth, her eyes open in surprise.

"Why did you do that, Emma? Why?"

"I was trying to throw it in the sink," she said. "I didn't mean it."

"Okay, Emma," I sighed and pulled myself upright. But it wasn't okay, because I confess, part of me didn't believe her.

August 3, 1967

MY MOTHER IS NOT DELUSIONAL, just asleep, although sometimes that can be the same thing. She thrashes as I stand above her, repeating the word "no" as she shakes her whole body along with her head. I put the bundle of roses at the foot of her bed, freeing my hands to hold hers.

"Mom," I say gently. "It's okay."

"No," she continues, "no."

Her damp hair, parted low, clings to one side of her face, obscuring one eye. When I reach up to brush it away, she swats at my hand. I go to the bathroom and dampen a washcloth, not the standard-issue ones stacked on the toilet tank, but one of the plush ones I brought last week and hid in the metal cabinet.

The cool cloth calms her for a second; her head stops turning and her breath becomes deep. When she speaks, I jump a little, as if I'd forgotten she was alive.

"If you don't stop this, you'll regret it," she growls.

I lift the cloth above her head.

"I'll make you pay," she says.

"Make who pay, Mom?"

"Mark my words, P.S. Mark my words."

When she wakes up, it's as if she doesn't know me. I try

to tell her about my trip to the doctor, but she gets a far-away look in her eyes. Half an hour later, after we have tea, she has no recollection of what she said when I arrived, and brushes it aside. I tell her she said it in a different voice, as if she was restaging something someone had said to her.

"Like playacting?" she says brightly, and I say yes. Then she asks me if she's ever told me the story of how she won the lead in her high school play. And even though I know it by heart, every nuance of how she found out the name of the play in advance, and memorized all the lines for her audition, I say no, Mom, tell me how you did it.

And that is the end of it. When I mention it to the nurse later, she tells me that dementia patients often remember things in their dreams that they can't remember awake, things that they have shoved aside, things that hurt, things they can't bear to recall.

I dillydallied quite a bit scheduling my next outing with
Ellie; the truth was, I didn't want to face Tinsley. All that
week after we'd seen her on the running path, I'd gone back
over practically every evening I'd spent with her, scanning
them for pieces of discontent, for frowns or pursed lips or un-
eaten meals, rooting around in my memory like photographs
in attic trunks.

Certainly, I'd always liked her on the surface, that's no
secret. The night we met, at that café on the Schuylkill River
Tom insisted upon, she was dressed very low key, in beige
slacks and a cream sweater, as if she knew she could rely on
her personality for color. She laughed easily and tolerated
Theo's serious and plodding questions, even teasingly asking him if he was interviewing her. I didn't think it was the
champagne cocktails fueling her, but her own engine, her
own power. Tom smiled and said so little I was afraid he
might be ill. By the time we'd ordered coffee and chocolate
mousse, I could see what Tom was up to. He was just letting her shine, not getting in the way. Not trying too hard
to play matchmaker—not after all the brooding intellectual
girlfriends he'd brought home who we didn't like. He knew

he'd hit pay dirt, and he just let it become apparent to us. And of course it worked.

Who wouldn't want a happy, friendly, curious daughter-in-law? Now I wonder if Tinsley was too friendly—if that's what got her into trouble.

I thought of other dinners we'd had together, and of course their wedding, barely a year after Theo died, and the lovely tribute Tom gave him with Tinsley looking on adoringly. The day Ellie was born, the christening, Thanksgiving and Christmas, the birthday dinners. In my mind's eye Tinsley is smiling in all of them. Even lately, when she chides me about Ellie, these little run-ins over diet or curfew or for discussing the family medical history, I don't get the sense that she is completely frowning on the other end of the phone. It's a happy kind of complaining, surely? Or is she fed up with the entire family? Not just Tom, but Tom's mother?

I called Tom at the office and reached him just before he got on a train to New York. I asked whether I could see Ellie Saturday morning. He said he thought it would be okay, but he'd have to look at something called the "family calendar" and confirm. I thought about asking him to come to breakfast with us then realized, sharply, that that would give Tinsley more time alone. Was that why she agreed to our playdates, at all? To help with her assignations?

At least I could be relatively certain Tom would be there when I picked up his daughter. His little rule was that he'd always be back from his trips by Saturday morning.

When I arrived I'd barely lifted my hand to knock when Ellie pulled the heavy door away from my knuckles. She must have been sitting on the bench in the foyer, waiting.

"Well, good morning to you," I said.

"I'm ready," she said, grinning and gesturing to a puffy vest that was meant to suffice for a coat.

"Indeed you are." I smiled and decided not to ask what on earth she planned to do if her arms and legs felt an unseasonable chill, and not her chest. I looked past her, toward the slice of kitchen visible from where I stood. I saw dishes in the drainer, rubber gloves. No parents.

"Where's your father?"

"He's in New York."

I frowned; Tom had broken his rule? "Really? What about your mother?"

"She's in the bathroom."

"Is she bathing?"

"No, silly! She's brushing her teeth."

Tinsley's phone vibrated on the kitchen island like a trapped June bug. I watched it scuttle about, and leaned over to steady it.

"Run and tell your mother we're leaving," I said, and the moment her back was turned, I whisked the phone into my purse.

"Well," Tinsley said and smiled widely as she ascended the steps, "where are we off to today?"

Her teeth, which had always been large, gleamed post-brushing and suddenly struck me as ridiculous. I couldn't take my eyes off them as we spoke—they were comical, a parody of a mouth.

I endured reexplaining myself: that we were going to the orchard. That there would be cider and strawberry picking. That it was right off Westchester Pike past the place where

Theo and I had always bought corn. I left out the part about their famous cider doughnuts—I didn't care to be admonished again for feeding her child sugar.

"Strawberry picking, huh?" Tinsley replied, ruffling Ellie's hair. "But Westchester Pike—isn't that kind of a long drive?"

I picked at the edge of my purse. It was my turn to speak in slow motion.

"Why do you ask, Tinsley?" I said, pulling out every syllable. "Do you need *extra time* for something today?"

I met her eyes, and to her credit, she didn't look away. But she didn't look angry, either; she looked at me the way women have looked at each other in locker rooms, in ballrooms, in drawing rooms since the beginning of time. She looked as if she was sizing up a rival.

"No," she said, too late.

"Well then." I smiled, a small smile, graceful, just a hint of teeth. "We'll see you . . . later. Give Tom my love."

At the orchard we went on a hayride through the farm and Ellie whispered, "Are there seat belts?" I told her just to hold on to the edge of the truck and the look on her face when we first took off was a mix of fear and joy. The freedom of her body, the swaying and bouncing, not held back by restraint. It was like seeing an astronaut's first weightlessness in space. *This is childhood, Ellie!* I wanted to shout above the children's squeals. This is all it is, so much and so little. My father and I took a hayride every year to pick pumpkins. We'd walk down every row in the patch, and he'd pick up vine after vine to look beneath it, trying to find the smallest pumpkins for our fairy gardens. The last things we'd add before the winter took them away. And in the spring, we picked strawberries together, too, not from an orchard, but from our own land, out past the gazebo, just short of our neighbor's stables. We always stopped to give a strawberry or two to their horses.

There were no horses at this orchard, though, and we walked into the barn and looked at displays of fruit carvings—elaborate faces that dried and fell into themselves, sunken apple cheekbones, tiny apple dimples. That's how I will look in five years, I thought. I let her eat not one, but *three* cider doughnuts because she said they were the most delicious thing she'd ever tasted. She wanted to take some home for her father, but I advised against it.

"Your mother would not like that," I said.

"My mother is ridiculous," she said, crumbs flying as the words came out.

I laughed and told her everyone thought their own mother was ridiculous.

"You loved your mother," she said. "We drank a toast to her."

"Well, when I was a girl I didn't appreciate her as much."

I thought of my mother's life after my father left; dressed up and going out to country clubs night after night when she lived at Aunt Caro's. The earnest men in blue blazers she introduced me to at Christmas or Thanksgiving, men she dated for meals. Thinking of her shining face as they poured her a glass of sherry turns my stomach to this day.

We agreed to bring home a pint of strawberries instead of the cider doughnuts, and as I was digging in my purse, Tinsley's phone bobbed to the surface.

"Did you pick up my mom's phone by accident?" Ellie asked.

Her words shot straight to my heart. You don't lie to a child like Ellie.

"No," I replied.

"Did you get a new phone like hers?" she asked as we wove our way through the bales and bushels to our car.

I got into the car and started the engine.

"Ellie," I said slowly, "I was worried that there might be a reason your mother never lets you touch her phone."

She blinked. "Like because there are naughty pictures on there?"

Good lord, that had never occurred to me! It's a sad day when your granddaughter knows more about pornography than you do.

"Uh, actually," I stalled, knowing I was getting into dangerous territory. Maybe a half lie wouldn't hurt? "I thought perhaps it's broken. Perhaps I should check it."

"But, Grandma?"

"Yes, dear?"

"That's a BlackBerry. Do you even know how to work it?"

"Well . . ."

She held out her hand. "It turns on fine," she said.

"Good," I said. "Is there some sort of . . . directory? Of names and numbers?"

"Here are her contacts right here."

"Wonderful!" I said and took the phone away before she stumbled on to something she shouldn't. I scrolled down through them, the way I'd seen Ellie do, and Tom and Tinsley, for that matter, a thousand times. But there weren't that many names on it—and most of them I remembered from the wedding and baby showers. Interestingly, there were no men other than Tom.

"Well, it seems to be working just fine," I said as I got down to the end and saw the name "Zoe." It struck me as an odd name for someone of Tinsley's generation. Someone younger, Ellie's age, perhaps.

"Do you have a friend named Zoe?" I asked her.

She shook her head, and didn't mention her mother having one, either.

I had to stop for gas before I dropped Ellie at home, and I sent her into the mini-mart for a candy bar while I sneaked over to the pay phone. It was covered with graffiti and the metal cord was bent unnaturally. Please work, I thought as I tossed in my quarter and dialed the number listed under "Zoe." The call was answered on the second ring.

"This is Zachary," he said. "Hello? Anyone there?"

I hung up the phone and sighed. The breath in my chest felt so deep it was painful. I hadn't really wanted to be right this time.

When I dropped Ellie off, I slipped Tinsley's phone back into the pocket of a coat that was hanging in the foyer. It felt as if I was concealing a weapon.

August 12, 1967

no bath

THE NURSING HOME SAID I should come right away. I
dialed Aunt Caro and she offered to pick me up. I assured
her that I was fine to drive, but she hesitated on the line, as
if she didn't want to hang up. Finally she added, "Ann, do you
want me to call Frank?"

My father's name was jarring and heavy in the air; no
one had said it in years. My mother simply called him "your
father." Half name, half accusation. He belongs to you, not
me. You're responsible for him now.

"Wh—"

"Ann," she said patiently, "don't you think he'd want to
know?"

"Why?" I spat through my tears. "So he can try to strip
her of something else? So he could take her death away from
her, too?"

She sighed a long sigh. It was heavy and full of something
she wasn't saying. "Maybe, dear, he'd like to clear the air."

"Apologize?"

"Perhaps, or certainly expl—"

"He should apologize to you," I said. Apologize to the
woman who had to pay for the last round of cancer special-

ists, the nursing home, the clothes, everything, since he left.

"No, dear, to her, to you, of course."

"You're a very optimistic woman, Aunt Caro." I sighed and hung up the phone. You had to be optimistic to lose both your sisters to cancer and not fall to the ground weeping. I called Betsy, then Theo, and to his credit, he didn't mention meetings or clients, and said to tell Betsy he'd be back on the next train.

Outside my mother's room, Aunt Caro stood in the corridor, looking intently at something on the wall. When I got closer I saw it was a watercolor of a cardinal in a tree.

"I guess you knew she loved birds."

I nodded. "That's why she wouldn't let me have a cat."

"She asked for this portrait to be moved here. It used to be near the nurses' station." She picked it up off the wall. "She's already gone," she said softly.

"Oh, no," I sobbed.

She put down the painting and held me tightly. The gesture was kind and loving, but it only served to make me aware that she wasn't my mother. No one holds you like your mother. No one ever will.

The door to the room was open an inch; I could see only a bedpost and a strip of wallpaper.

"Was she alone? I mean when—"

"The nurse claims she was with her."

"Claims?" It was just like Aunt Caro to kick up a little trouble.

"I think they say that to make people feel better. I think it's in the nursing home manual." She sighed and looped an arm around my shoulder, releasing a puff of Chanel No. 5 mixed with hair spray.

"Do you remember those exquisite bird houses Frank made for her?"

"Please, Aunt Caro. I don't want to—"

"She loved all beautiful things, which was her undoing."

I squeezed her hand. Why is it that everyone labels something one loves as one's undoing, when it's only illness, betrayal, death, or divorce that truly undoes anything?

"My father was her undoing," I said.

"Dear, dear Ann," she sighed.

I went inside. The pink roses I'd brought earlier in the week were still fragrant at her bedside. Some of them were wilted, gone soft at the stem, and their petals littered the tabletop. But if I could still smell them, I hoped she could, too.

"Oh, Mom," I whimpered, and a bolt of pain shot through my right side. It connected us, that pain, like a string of Christmas lights, an electric current. It went through us both, from my breast to hers, past her mattress, the floor, into the earth. My cancer was gone, but hers came back. She could have lived three more months or three more years, they'd told us. Nobody thought it might be three weeks.

When I brushed my lips across her cheek, she didn't smell like herself, she smelled like the room, like roses. That was death, I thought; you became something else altogether, an envelope that held parts of other people, what they remembered of you, what they wished you were.

An hour later, when I stepped out of the lobby, grateful for air, my father was like a bear in the parking lot. My breath caught in my throat at the sight of his brown suit, his broad back, leaning against a burgundy Cadillac. No cigar, but when I got closer I smelled one in his pocket.

"It's too late," I said, and he turned around. His car was new and gleaming, recently polished. His suit, with its wide lapels and even wider tie, looked completely of the moment, which angered me. My mother had worn her sister's hand-me-downs for years.

"Well, I tried," he said.

"Where do you live that you arrived here so quickly?"

He opened his mouth and I held up a hand. "Don't answer," I said. "I don't really want to know."

"How are the children?"

"How are your grandchildren, you mean? They're fine. They're just dandy," I said tartly.

"I don't know why," he sighed, "after all these years, you persist in believing only your mother's version of the events."

"Looked pretty black and white to me."

"Did it ever occur to you that she—"

"That she what, Dad? That she was responsible? That she, I don't know, cheated on you down at the club because you were a bastard and she was lonely? Yes, that occurred to me. But it's not true. And even if it was, nothing gives you license to do what you did. Nothing. The woman is dead. And now I don't have any parents."

I turned away, taking long, half-running steps toward my car.

"Annie! Ann-o!"

"Don't," I said, whirling toward him. "Don't ever call me that."

"Let me explain. Now that you're grown, perhaps—"

"Caro shouldn't have called you," I said. He was still standing in the parking lot, hands on his hips—like a fat, petulant child, like a little girl—when I pulled away.

When I got home the baby was napping and Emma was coloring in her room. When I asked if they'd been good for him, Theo said they'd been angels.

"Angels," I repeated. It was an interesting choice of words. I looked up at Theo to see if he looked sorry for that misstep, and he did. His eyes were wide, and his mouth was pulled in a straight line—small and uncertain, as if he just didn't know what to say.

"All things considered, your mother had a good life," he said.

I shook my head. I knew he didn't know what to say. But I didn't believe that platitude; I never would. She was fifty-three and died with no money and no husband. She spent the last months of her life with a rotting body and a rotting mind, believing the nursing home was a pied-à-terre and that she would be going back to "the main house" any day. She thought I was her friend from college, not her daughter. When Aunt Caro visited, she called her Louise, the name of her maid, and handed her things that needed to be mended.

"She didn't have a life; she had an existence," I said. "She didn't even have the memory of a life," I said, tears streaming down my face.

Theo stepped in and hugged me hard. It felt strange to be held so tightly now, one breast crushed and the other side untouched. It was like being half held, not really held at all.

August 16, 1967

bubble bath

THE POST-FUNERAL GATHERING was supposed to be a
lunch, but a dozen people stayed at Aunt Caro's house until
six, drinking all her scotch. Most of my friends, including
Betsy, had left by three, so there was a long stretch of weary
politeness. The tea sandwiches were long gone; the trays
with only doilies and parsley looked naked and sad. Like seeing a kitchen's skin and bones.

"We're in danger of needing to make peanut butter
sandwiches," Caro said, sipping a vodka, and slid into her
favorite wing chair, finally unoccupied. "Don't you want a
drink, Ann?" She clinked her ice cubes at me, as if to wake
me up.

"If I start drinking," I said, looking at my watch, "who
will convince them to leave?"

"That's twisted logic, Ann. What do sober people know
about drunks?"

My mother's old friends weren't drunks, per se. They
were drinking opportunists. A funeral provided a perfect
storm of opportunity: a reason to toast, an open bar, and a
perfect excuse if you happened to overindulge or misbehave.

"Has Theo gone as well?"

"He went home to spell the babysitter. She had to leave at four."

She sipped her drink slowly and nodded. "I'm glad you found someone, Ann," she said softly.

"What?" I said, startled.

"Someone to babysit."

"Oh," I said, and relief flooded me. "Yes, it's that young woman from Emma's school. The one who's so good with her."

"God bless anyone who works with children. I couldn't do it."

"I don't think I could, either. Some days . . . well, just having two is too much."

"From what I've seen of Emma, having one is sometimes too much."

I sat forward in my chair. "What do you mean?"

"She's a handful, is what I mean."

"Do you think so? I mean, it's not just me, she seems—"

"Difficult?"

"Well, yes. The pediatrician says she's fine, the teachers say she's intelligent, but . . ." I shook my head. "Everyone thinks she's just jealous of the baby. Acting out, that's all. The terrible threes, I suppose. This, too, shall pass, they say."

She nodded and swirled the ice in her drink with one manicured finger. "Well, I only had one, and it was a boy, so what do I know?"

I nodded my head. My cousin William was athletic, smart, fun. He'd grown from a golden child into a golden adult—he was the head of a pharmaceutical company. Aunt Caro and Uncle Billy had never seemed to worry about him, although he wasn't married and traveled constantly and was always going on vacations that sounded vaguely dangerous. I'd last seen him a few years ago at Uncle Billy's funeral and my mother told me she was certain he was homosexual. I'd laughed at her. William looked like all the architects at Theo's office—polished loafers, nicely cut suits. Shirts that coordinated perfectly with their ties. It sounded like a joke: what was the difference between an architect and a homosexual?

"But," she added, "it's no fun waiting for it to pass, is it?"

I shook my head. When I'd told Emma her grandmother had died she'd asked who killed her. A person didn't kill her, cancer killed her, I said. I sat on the edge of her bed and waited for the questions a normal child would ask: What's cancer? Where is Grandma now? But they didn't come. No more questions, no tears. She stared at a spot on her wall, then reached up to pick it off. She seemed angry when she realized it wasn't dimensional, pulling at it with her nail long after someone else would have given up. Well, I thought, she's determined, anyway. After she fell asleep I thumbed through the picture book on her bedside table, scanning the pages about a family of flowers to see if the word "kill" was in it. To see if a vine strangled the baby rose. If an evil gardener chopped its blossomy head off.

Aunt Caro and I sat for a few minutes while she finished her drink, then she asked if I wanted to look at some old pictures, to reminisce, and I said no.

"It's too sad looking at everything she used to have," I said. "She was so happy in all those photos."

"A person has to learn to be happy in all circumstances," she said quietly.

"I think she did, to some degree."

"I did what I could, Ann. Within sensible limits, I—"

"Aunt Caro, that's not what I'm saying. I'm just saying the photos make me sad, that's all. It's going to be years before I can look at them again."

She nodded slowly. "If you look carefully, Ann," she added, "you'll see she's not always happy in the photos."

I blinked. "That can't be true."

"Look carefully," she said quietly, and we watched her guests pick at the trays, as if they were considering eating the wet doilies, too.

Betsy called and suggested I take Ellie ice skating. Said there was a new rink open near the old township building, and that there was rumored to be a disco ball and something called laser tag, which sounded just dreadful. Usually Betsy is the friend who reminds me of how easy it is to break a hip, and that I should stop using bath oils in the tub, so I was starting to wonder about the state of her aging brain.

"Well, I used to be quite good, as you know, but I haven't skated in years," I mused.

"Oh, Ann, I said you should take her there, not that you should skate, too. Dear lord!"

"Well, what fun would that be?"

"You could give her pointers."

I wrinkled my nose; I remembered trying to teach my daughter to skate when I was pregnant with Tom; I'd call out instructions from the sidelines and she'd travel two steps and then flop down like Bambi, legs akimbo. When she got up, she glared at me as if I were an instrument of the devil. No; the only way to teach them was to skate along backward and hold their hands in front of you.

Who knows, maybe Betsy is finally losing it after all those years of smart and steady. Maybe she got tired of always being right, of always having the answer, of always knowing what was best. When my mother died, she was the only one who understood. She stood with me at the grave site and held me as I sobbed. I kept saying I didn't expect it to hurt so much; I didn't know why, with her death imminent for so long, that it affected me so. And she said, "It hurts because when your mother dies, your whole childhood disappears. It's as if it never happened."

Betsy could have been a psychologist or a priest, but now she's telling seventy-year-olds to go to ice-skating rinks, and last week she actually bought a contraption that allows her to play tennis on her television set via some sort of handheld device. When I stopped by on Wednesday, she was swinging a white remote in the air and complaining about her backhand. Through the window it looked as if she'd taken up interpretive dance.

Though I hadn't been on ice skates in many years, I reluctantly mentioned it as an option to Ellie, in a list that included bowling, pottery painting, and going to the movies. When she hesitated I was afraid I'd have to think of a new list of things; I supposed if push came to shove we could always play tennis on Betsy's TV.

"Can't I just come over?" Ellie said.

"Well, certainly," I said, relieved. "We'll make a collage, or bake cookies, or do a jigsaw puzzle."

When Tom dropped her off, she headed straight to the puzzle on the dining room table with barely a hello. I asked how he was, how work was going, specifically, and he simply said he was busy, and so was Tinsley—she was training for a marathon.

"Well, make sure she doesn't run too far," I said quietly.

He sighed. "That's the whole point of a marathon, Mother—running twenty-six miles."

"I'm well aware of what a marathon is, Tom."

He seemed tired, so I didn't push things. After I waved good-bye, I vowed to be less meddling, subtler.

The puzzle was of a lake filled with ducks, and it was difficult—the water and the birds were all the same brackish color; the pieces of waves and feathers all looked vaguely alike. Ellie frowned after she'd laid in all the corners—it was hard to know where to begin. I suggested she look for pieces that contained both duck feathers and water—that way she could build heads and wings onto bottoms. But after half an hour, we'd built only two ducks and had no idea where they belonged on the lake.

"You'd think they could have thrown in a red rowboat or something," I muttered.

"Grandma, can we play in the attic?" Her face shone brightly, as if the word attic was "ice cream." I felt a flush, too, as I always did, I'd noticed, whenever she called me Grandma.

"Play dress up? I don't have much clothing up there, you know."

"No, just, you know, like, look through the old trunks like we did before, on your mom's birthday."

In the last week she seemed to have added "you know" and "like" to her sentences, the same way the college students did.

"Okay, but it will be hot up there."

"I don't care."

"We're going to need some beverages, I believe."

"Coke?" she whispered conspiratorially.

"Let's get the ice cubes and the jelly jars," I replied, and headed for the kitchen.

There were two chairs in the attic from the last time. I brought up a portable fan, cranked open the windows on each side, and we settled in with our drinks, taking care to stay away from the green trunks. I read her a few letters Theo had written me while we were engaged; she got a huge kick out of his misspelled words. I explained to her that architects were like mad scientists—no time for frivolities like spelling or nuisances like cooking, cleaning, mowing the lawn. It was all about the projects—their babies, their life. Ellie said that sounded like too much work. She said her father always mowed the lawn, and I smiled, then frowned. I hated hearing ways in which Tom didn't take after Theo; it brought back all the old worries. Over the years, I'd make mental lists of all the ways in which they were alike: their blue eyes, their love of art and music, their quietness and seriousness. At night I'd count them like sheep, willing them, bonding them. When Tom chose to be a lawyer, I tried to talk him into architecture, which he'd always admired. As if I could change all things by changing one thing.

Under Tom's christening gown and baby book was a box of buttons, which I'd completely forgotten about. Ellie took them out and surveyed them, like marbles. My mother and Aunt Caro had collected buttons as children—many of them were antique, made of glass or bone and other things that are probably legislated against and outlawed now. Ellie held up one that appeared to be alligator, and said, "Wow."

"We should do something with those, I suppose." I sighed. "Sew them onto a felted purse or something. Betsy might have some ideas. She thought I should teach you to knit this winter."

"Or you could just put the buttons in a glass jar on your coffee table," Ellie said.

"Well, that would be easier, wouldn't it?"

I took a sip of my Coke while Ellie crouched above the brown trunk. She set the box of buttons on the floor and pulled out a rolled-up calendar from 1962 with photos of office buildings.

"Oh, that's Theo's. Are his office things in there, too? I didn't look in this trunk."

"Yes," she said, pulling out a red stapler and a leather pencil cup that had a mechanical pencil and paper clip still in it.

"Are there blueprints in there? We could make wrapping paper from them. I did that now and then with your father. That would be fun, wouldn't it?"

When Ellie pulled up the woven basket, I had no idea whose it was. I remembered the leather pencil cup, but not this. She opened the lid and we both expected, and hoped for, something else. I expected paper clips. She probably hoped for coins, buried treasure.

She pulled out two rubber ducks, one larger than the other. The fan swept across my back, calves, ankles, oscillating so hard that I went cold. The Coke fizzed in my throat, threatening, and I held my hand over my mouth.

"Are these my dad's?"

I closed my eyes slowly and willed myself to nod. If I didn't open my eyes, maybe I wouldn't see any more, or say any more. Maybe I wouldn't have to lie to the child I didn't ever want to lie to.

"A mama and a baby duck," she said.

"Yes," I whispered and swallowed. "Put those away now, Ellie," I said. "They're very fragile."

"Okay," she said uncertainly.

"Are you sure there aren't any blueprints?"

"Well, there's a bunch of tubes."

"Take those out instead, why don't you?"

I heard the rustling and I opened my eyes. But I still saw the bright yellow of those floating ducks and the way their blue eyes had faded, peeled off beneath not Tom's fingers but Emma's, Emma of the tangled hair and tantrums, the child who never looked like a child unless she was asleep. At her funeral, that's what struck me most—that she looked peaceful and sweet, almost elegant in death. A way she had so rarely presented herself to me in life. It was graceful, almost, to say good-bye to her in that state. I stood over her coffin and thought she had never looked so happy. But when I heard a man say, "She's at peace now," over my shoulder, I whirled around as if prepared to pounce. My father stood in front of me, with Theo just behind him, looking sheepish.

"Will you excuse me? I think I'm going to be ill," I said, and ran outside. Predictably, my father followed me, not Theo.

He waited in the parking lot, fifty feet away, and watched as I tucked my feet beneath me and sat at the edge of the wooded lot, picking tufts of grass out of the ground and throwing them.

He stepped toward me; I heard his heavy feet on the gravel.

"Don't come any closer," I said.

"Ann, I can't imagine what you're going through—"

"No, you can't."

"I just wanted to say—"

"That you're sorry?"

"Well, yes."

I turned and shook the last pieces of grass off my black skirt. "Daddy," I said slowly, "I hope you're sorry for the rest of your life."

There was more I could have said, and might have, if I hadn't seen Betsy appear outside the funeral parlor door. If she had stepped outside a minute earlier, she might have stopped me from going as far as I did.

My father turned to see where I was looking. Emboldened, knowing there was a witness, he walked up to me and took an envelope out of his breast pocket.

"Whatever that is, I don't want it."

"Annie," he said, his face contorting as he tried to stop the tears. "What do I have to do for you to forgive me? Please, just read this."

The envelope's paper was thick and starchy, and when his tears dropped on it, they looked as big as raindrops.

I took the envelope without a word, and when I got home, cracked it open just far enough to recognize the loops of his familiar handwriting, then threw it away.

That was the last time I saw him. When he died five years later, I didn't go to his funeral. His new wife, Bitte, sent me the small check from his estate, and I put it in an account for Tom. I didn't even send her a condolence card.

"Grandma, are you okay?" Ellie asked, and I said yes,

clearing my throat. I waited a few seconds, swallowing, then said why don't we go downstairs and make something out of those blueprints?

As we sat at the dining room table and made book jackets for her textbooks, she stopped suddenly and looked up.

"I found something strange in my house yesterday, too. And not in the attic, either."

"Really?" I smiled, pouring her more Coke.

"I found a red Villanova sweatshirt."

"That doesn't sound so strange."

"It's not my dad's."

I met her eyes. "How do you know?"

"He hates red, and he went to Penn."

"Well, it could be your mother's."

She shook her head. "It's huuuuge."

"Babysitter?"

"I asked Lauren and she said no."

"There's probably a logical explanation."

"Yeah, just like there is for the kissing."

"Ellie," I said, taking her hands in mine, "your mother loves you. And there are far worse things she could have done to you or to anyone else than, than—"

"Than kissing a friend."

"Yes," I said. "So let's not think about it anymore."

"My friend Courtney says I should use it to blackmail her for an iPod."

"I think I'd like to meet Courtney," I said and smiled. The mood lightened, but the word "blackmail" hung in the air, dark and silty.

August 22, 1967

bubble bath

HE CALLED WHEN THE CHILDREN were napping. He is
thoughtful that way.

He'd read about my mother's death in the paper, and he
said the same thing he'd said the last time he called: When
were you going to tell me, Annie? As if we were still high
school sweethearts at the private schools across the street
from each other, and I owed him information about my life,
my family, the events of my day. Back then we shared grades,
scores, gossip. He'd always wanted detail—what was your
time in the relay? How many people were at the pep rally?
Now I'd had a baby and not told him. I'd lost my mother and
not told him. I don't know what he had for breakfast or what
color shirt he is wearing. What else don't I know? He doesn't
know I lost my breast as well as my mother, and I don't know
how to tell him that.

"I want to see you," he says, holding on to the word "you"
like a glider, moving across the pitch of towers and monu-
ments and cupolas, west to where I stand in a shuttered
upstairs window with the beige phone cord curled around
one hand. Can he imagine he sees my roofline, Theo's deck
where he takes his coffee, the whitewashed brick chimney,

the tree that brushes it out back, the wrens that flit through its branches, and all the houses, the woods, hills, wires, everything in between, that separate us?

The last time I was in the city, I drove past Peter's office building, a tall silver scar, circling the block for nearly an hour, watching the revolving glass door, the way it pulled people in in slow motion and spit them back out again. He didn't come out. I didn't go in. The taste of disappointment in my mouth reminded me of the day I'd waited for my father. The city blocks weren't like mine, filled with neighbors and an occasional college student, where I could hear the drag and slide of their guitar cases and blue jeans brushing against the sidewalk. No. This was all clicking briefcase and honking horn. I felt frumpy even hidden in my car.

"How about this afternoon?" I say and he is stunned, quiet for a second. He expected protest, impossibility. "I have a sitter coming at four."

We agreed to meet at four thirty, at a grimy tavern not far from the train station. I'd thought of Stuart's first, but it was too popular. No one we knew had ever gone to the tavern—I'd lived in the area my entire life and never been. All I knew was that it used to be called the Lamplighter, but now it had a cheap sign that simply said TAVERN. I tried not to dress too carefully; didn't want the babysitter to think anything was off. I wore a red silk blouse with plain gray slacks, and low heels. At the last minute I added a woven Tibetan belt Betsy had given me; it looked like something a hitchhiker would wear until you put it on, until you saw what joy a new texture could add. I decided not to put my red lipstick on until I got in the car. When Emma's teacher asked where

I was going, and did I want to leave a number? I said I was running errands, that Theo could be reached at his office in an emergency. I kissed the baby, and when I tried to hug Emma, she squirmed away, preferring her teacher.

"You're so good with her," I said softly, and they both smiled. I felt no guilt leaving, not one bit. Only later would I feel guilty over not feeling guilty.

I arrived first and chose a booth near the jukebox. Two men sat at the bar drinking beer near the neon PABST sign; they didn't turn when I came in. Good, I thought; I wasn't dressed too flashily. After a few minutes the bartender walked over, snapped a coaster down, and asked what I'd like to have. I looked up into his soft cushion of a face, took in his faint scent of beer and eggs, and was tempted, for just a second, to tell him all the things I wanted to have. A staff of four, a husband who was always home to help. A daughter who loved me back. But I smiled and said a Manhattan, please, and one for my friend. I tripped a little over the word "friend" and his eyebrows went up.

"An imaginary friend?" He smiled, and I said no, he'd be here in a second, and just then Peter walked in the door. His sport coat held the smell of the outside world—clear and fragrant. When I hugged him I held on to one of his lapels, trying to memorize the feel of the linen in my hand.

"Look at you." He smiled as he sat down.

"That's a silly phrase, isn't it? I can't look at myself."

"You look terrific."

"I wish I felt more terrific."

"Was it terrible? Your mother's funeral?"

"No. Yes. My father showed up."

I realized as the words slipped out that I hadn't told anyone else.

"Oh, Ann, I don't know what to say, let alone feel—was it okay? Were you glad to see him?"

My chest heaved. "No."

"How is his health? He was always so hale and hearty."

I smiled ruefully; I'd stopped trying to picture my father when I was young, but I could remember Peter and my father together, waiting in front of the big stone fireplace for me to come downstairs in my sweater set and pearls. My father nursing a highball in one hand and leaning over to stoke the fire with the other. Putting the poker down and standing up to his full height, with Peter so much smaller, so much less manly in comparison that he looked like some prey my father had shot and brought home to mount.

"We didn't actually converse."

"All these years, Ann, and you don't talk?"

"He just felt guilty. That's all it was—he came because he feels guilty."

Peter took my hand across the table. "I still can't believe it, after all this time. It doesn't make sense to me."

I shrugged. "He's selfish, feels guilty, and wants forgiveness. End of story."

"I did a story for *Esquire,* a few years back, about rich men who hide their assets from their wives in divorces. I guess I was inspired by Frank, who knows. Anyway, the profile of these guys—well, your father doesn't fit it. These guys are heartless, they're sociopaths . . . He just . . . it doesn't fit. I really liked your dad. I've never been so wrong about anyone in my life. It will never make sense."

"No, I suppose not," I said. I closed my eyes, shook my head, as if I could empty myself of all the memories. "Let's talk about something else, shall we?"

"Have I ever told you," he said, "that you always reminded me of a bird?"

"What?"

"You know how Greggy Peterson always had that sheepdog hair? And how Mina Bellows had eyes like a tabby cat?"

"Yes." I smiled, remembering our classmates and the endless conversations about them.

"You're like a beautiful little bird."

"Am I?" My smile widened as I leaned down to sip my drink. I wondered if I'd always been birdlike; if that's the quality my mother adored; if that's why my father made the bird houses.

He nodded toward my blouse. "Robin redbreast," he said and smiled.

My tears were involuntary and instantaneous, as if he'd turned on a spigot. He misinterpreted them at first, holding my hand and telling me my mother was a lovely woman, that she'd lived through difficult times with honor and dignity. That he was sorry he'd brought up my father, that he didn't mean to dredge up old memories.

I held up one hand to stop him, and finally, I laughed.

"Did I say something funny?"

I shook my head. There were so many things to be sad about; how could he know? And he held his own sadness; my mother had loved Peter, had fawned over him, giggled like a schoolgirl at his jokes. When we broke up, she was sadder than either of us, and never ceased to ask if I'd seen him, or heard word of him, whenever I ran into someone from Langley. And she kept the pictures of the two of us in her album, instead of slicing him off the way Betsy's mother had unceremoniously removed her old beaux. Peter, I knew, had loved my mother, too.

"Peter," I said, "it's not just my mother, there's more."

And then, slowly, with both tears and laughter safely at bay, I told him about my breast surgery. I must have given him enough details to satisfy him, because he didn't ask questions, and his eyes, god bless him, his eyes didn't go to my chest like some people's do. They stayed with me, eye to eye.

And then he did it again, as he had last year at our high school reunion. Once again, he said the perfect thing at the perfect time.

"Oh, Annie. How can I miss what's gone when what you have left is so beautiful?"

That's not when our evening ended, but that's the last thing I remember him saying: the perfect thing. Everything else that came after, the small talk, the we should do this again, the aren't the cheeseburgers delicious, the call me next week, paled in comparison. He kissed me good-bye, just once, on the lips, and I felt that same electricity. It would never go away; it would run between us always, over hill and dale, through drought and famine, month to year to decade. It was a fact, not a feeling, and I had to accept it.

When I got home I went up to tuck in the baby. He was asleep, but I just wanted to look at him for a few seconds. Peter had asked me what day he was born. I could see him

counting backward, fingers tapping it out on the nicked lino-
leum table, the months, the weeks. I told him in no uncertain
terms that he was wrong. How do you know? he replied. How
can you be sure? "He has blue eyes," I said, looking straight
into Peter's brown.

Now the baby's long-lashed eyes were closed, and it was
as if I couldn't remember their hue. Had I conjured it up,
looked into them like a reflecting pool and seen what I'd
wanted to see?

When I'd walked in, Theo had tilted his face up from the
blueprints spread across the dining room table and sniffed
the air. Like a dog, I thought.

"You smell of smoke," he said, not distastefully.

"They should outlaw smoking in theaters," I said, and he
sniffed again.

He's a dog and I'm a bird and he'll forever be looking
for me, searching me out, wondering where I am. I went to
the kitchen and set the table for breakfast while Theo con-
centrated on his project. I don't think I'd ever noticed before
how much less handsome Theo was with his eyes downcast.
And they were always down now, aimed toward his blueprints, low to the ground, an animal not meant to fly.

September 2, 1967

no bath for three days

THE BABY WAS INCONSOLABLE the night before last. That's a word you just don't know the meaning of until you have children, is it? I was up with him at 2:00, at 3:15, and again at 4:00. I know he's teething, although I don't remember Emma going through this. It seems she always had teeth.

He didn't want his pacifier; didn't want a bottle; or teething biscuit, cereal, or cold spoon. I rubbed brandy on his bulging gums, but they stayed as red as a Monopoly house. I turned on the washing machine and set his basket near it, hoping it would lull him. He was momentarily startled into silence, then started to wail again. I felt my hands go into fists. I closed the door to the laundry room and took three steps away. Was the crying easier to take with the door between us? The muffling made it worse, as if I was choking him.

I took a deep breath and looked up at the ceiling. I wanted another wife in the house. Polygamy, I wanted polygamy. I wanted someone else to rock him, someone else to tell me it was okay, that every baby does this and every mother feels this. I wanted platitudes and rhymes and clichés. I wanted this, too, shall pass. I wanted, I realized with an ache, a mother. Not my mother, necessarily, with her flawed memory and pampered habits, but a smart one. A patient one. Maybe any mother would do.

I cried on one side of the door while the baby wailed on the other. Our sobs blended together, like a composite character, louder and less happy than either one of us alone. We both wanted our mothers, and neither of us had them.

Finally I blew my nose and opened the door. I picked him up and brought his wailing face as close to mine as my ears could stand; I needed to smell the beauty of his scalp, his skin. Even angry. Even loud. Even screeching, wailing like a lunatic, you are a miracle. What I used to say to Emma. Every child is a miracle, I would repeat over her tantrums. Every one.

It didn't help. "What do you want?" I cried. "What?"

I knew I couldn't stop it—I just had to endure it. Wasn't that what Betsy told me once? When you can't stop it, just endure it?

I rocked him and walked around the house, up the stairs, into his room. I watched his open mouth in the air. Opening and closing. Rooting for worms, like a baby bird. There was nothing else I could do, nothing left on the list. I unbuttoned my nightgown, and took out my left breast. It hadn't been used in weeks, and I had no reason to hope it would work. But he latched on and pulled, finding whatever was left of me. It must have been enough, because we fell asleep together that way, he and I, in our chair.

I didn't wake up until Emma opened the door. The sound of her in the room, her confusion and jealousy in the air, woke me up. I covered myself hastily and put the baby back in his crib.

The next day his tooth broke through. He woke up giggling and gurgling, and when I brought him downstairs, he sat happily in his high chair, banging on the metal tray with a spoon while I filled the percolator with coffee.

The phone rang and I frowned; only bad news came this early in the day. I was right: it was Sarah, the sitter, canceling for the afternoon and evening. She was sick, and I summoned sympathy for a minute or two, asked about her symptoms. But when I hung up the phone, I felt tears in my eyes. It had been a long few days. I needed a bath, fresh air, a drink. I needed an evening with Peter.

"Oh well," I said to the baby as I opened a jar of Gerber applesauce, "maybe there's a movie of the week on TV tonight, huh?" And he smiled. "Maybe I'll grow old and fat and stinky wearing the same nightgown forever," I said, and he smiled.

A few minutes later Emma came downstairs, and he smiled for her.

"He's showing off his tooth," I said.

She smiled at him, and he smiled back, and she giggled.

"We all have teeth now," she said, and I said, yes, you're right.

I patted her on the hand and couldn't help noticing her knuckles felt dry, scratchy. Maybe the bubble baths were drying out her skin again. Betsy had suggested baby oil in the bath instead, but that made it too slippery, and Emma always protested the lack of bubbles.

I set out Emma's raisin bran and orange juice and she rubbed her eyes and yawned.

"Is Daddy back from his trip?"

"No, honey. Do you want bacon? There's bacon in the oven and I can make you an egg."

She ate her cereal; that was my answer. Why did I expect anything more? My memories of my own childhood, I suppose; my mother cheery and me polite in our sunroom overlooking the pond. The calm stirring of sugar in tea, the sighing over the beauty of the day, the napkins always on our laps. The arrival of my father, freshly shaved, and the smell of his lime soap hovering over me as he kissed me on the forehead.

I turned to the sink to wash the bacon pan. When I heard it, at first I thought it was just the water I was running. And then, louder, a gurgling that was different. I spun around. My baby was gasping for air.

I yanked on the metal high chair tray, squeezing it until it popped and clattered to the floor. I pulled him up to my shoulder and hit him sharply on the back. He gagged and tears flew out suddenly, as if his ducts had been clogged and not his throat. I held him up in the air. His face was reversing itself, back into baby pink.

"Don't scare me like that," I said. My hands were shaking, and his chin buckled and quivered, as if in response.

I put him back in his high chair. As I turned away something dark caught my eye on the floor: three soggy raisins, plumped up by milk.

"Emma, did you throw these on the—"

I knelt to pick them up, then stopped dead in my tracks. I turned to her; our eyes locked and I knew. I just knew.

"You fed the baby? Emma, I told you, never give him anything, ever!"

"But, Mommy, he has a tooth!"

"That doesn't matter."

"He looked like he wanted my breakfast."

"Emma," I said evenly, "only mommies and daddies can feed babies. Not sisters. Not ever."

She ate her cereal silently, her eyes down, like Theo's.

"Look at me so I know that you heard me!"

Her eyes met mine, but they were as flat and dull as a lake. I picked the raisins off the floor and sat with her while she finished eating, struggling to think of something to say.

"Should we go for a walk later?" I asked, trying to sound upbeat. "After nap time? To the park?"

She shrugged her shoulders.

"Would you like to plant flowers? We could gather leaves and acorns and stones. We could make a fairy garden."

"I guess," she said, and I nodded, then cleared the plates away. Maybe she'd be more enthusiastic later.

At nap time, I pulled a crystal bell off the cabinet in the dining room, tied a ribbon around it, and hung it on the baby's door. If my daughter had been a cat, I think I would have hung one around her neck.

Downstairs I kicked off my shoes and picked up the front section of the paper, and a few minutes later I was asleep, too. Half an hour later, the doorbell woke me. Sarah? I thought hopefully, but no, it was Aunt Caro, carrying a small tote bag.

"Sorry I didn't call first. You look a fright."

"The baby's teething. I haven't slept."

"Well, I'd offer to help you but I'm miserable with babies. It's a miracle mine lived to adulthood."

"It's a miracle any of them do," I sighed, thinking of the raisins.

"I brought you some things of your mother's," she said. "They were in storage."

"Storage?" I blinked. "Where?"

"A safe-deposit box."

"No," I said, shaking my head, "she and I emptied that when she went into the nursing home. I have her pearls and her high school ri—"

"This is a second box."

I frowned.

"It was in my name," she said quietly. "I opened it for her when she started to think Frank was hiding assets."

I looked in the tote. A navy velvet ring box, a key, and a beige satin bag that looked as if it held lingerie. I lifted the lid of the box.

"An emerald ring?"

"Surely you don't remember it. Your mother rarely wore it."

"Why? It's so beautiful."

"I don't know," she said too quickly, with a wave of her hand. "Too big and gaudy." She picked at the hem of her skirt.

"It's not that big," I said, slipping it on my finger. The mounting curled slightly around each side of the stone, like a gold vine. "The setting reminds me of a sculpture," I said.

"Well, it's quite a bit of gold. You could sell it."

"Why would I do that?"

"Well, it has no real meaning. It's not as if your father gave it to her."

I sighed. "That wouldn't have much meaning, either, I'm afraid."

I took it off and twirled it to appreciate the setting of the intertwined gold, which was almost, well, floral.

"Who did give it to her?"

"No idea."

"Huh," I said, squinting. "Who's Rose?"

"What?"

"The inscription."

"What inscription?" She yanked it out of my hand.

"It says, 'To my rose.' Did Mom have any friends named Rose?"

"No idea," she said breezily, handing it back.

I picked up the key: LIPSKI FURRIERS.

"I thought she sold her mink."

"No. She kept it for you." She handed me the satin roll. "And this will help pay for the storage fees."

I unwrapped the roll, expecting more jewelry, but there was a stack of $100 bills, thirty of them. I looked up at my aunt, who shrugged.

"She said it was all she could gather up. After Frank left I told her to put it in the bank but she seemed to think he could still get his hands on anything that wasn't locked away."

"That must have been such a nightmare for her."

"She knew nothing about money. And clearly, neither did your father. I hope you haven't inherited this propensity."

I scowled. "He was the man who knew too much, I'd say."

"Ann," she said softly, "if you listen to nothing else I've ever told you, listen to this: the stock market is not a playpen."

I blinked. Was Aunt Caro going senile on me, too?

"She owed you money," I said, handing it back.

"She owed me nothing, Ann. Take it and go on vacation.

Or buy a savings bond for your children. I wish I'd remembered socking it away for her; you could have invested it."

She looked at her watch and asked what time Theo would be home. When I told her he was out of town, she raised her eyebrows and said, "Again?"

"Ann." She sighed as she headed for the door. "When I was your age, my husband fell in love with his assistant. I caught them kissing one afternoon when I stopped in his office for lunch."

"Really?"

"Yes, and here's the kicker—his assistant was a man."

"Aunt Caro!"

"Yes, that's where my son gets it, I suppose," she said, smiling. "But the reason I'm telling you this now is because I want you to know something else." She picked up her coat and stood at the door. "It all began when he started taking business trips. I don't think they were business trips at all."

"I don't think Theo—"

She held up her hand. "I'm not accusing. I'm just saying to keep your eyes open. Open the mail, look through the drawers. And always hang on to a little bit of your own money."

After Caro left, the rest of the evening passed without incident—we went to the park and Emma and I played hopscotch. The children ate dinner, Emma drank chocolate milk. We read stories, and after I put them to bed, I considered putting myself to bed. Instead, I picked up the heaping laundry basket and started folding. Socks, dungarees, boxer shorts. Always a million small pieces that needed to be put back together. It takes half an hour, maybe more, just to fold.

Upstairs, when I opened Theo's sock drawer, the drawer liner curled up on one side. I tried to smooth it down, and it protested.

Theo kept glue in the top drawer of his desk; when I opened the drawer I expected to find glue, and I did. But my aunt's words come back to me: keep your eyes open. I pulled the drawer out farther but then it stuck. Frowning, I reached my fingers underneath, and felt something familiar. A heavy paper, good for absorbing ink, thoughts, tears. It was rolled into a tight scroll, like a cigar. I pulled it out and took it into my room.

I slid off the old rubber band and unrolled the missing page of my diary.

MAY I7. MY HIGH SCHOOL REUNION.

It wasn't more complicated or mysterious than I have recalled. My entry didn't offer much more detail than my memory, but there was enough. Enough that Theo wanted to erase it, to cut it out of my heart, to keep me from remembering what I remembered.

MAY I7. MY HIGH SCHOOL REUNION.

I knew he would be there, just as I knew there would be punch and balloons. Who am I kidding? I went to see him, not anyone else. But I expected it to be different. I thought he would live farther away; I thought his wife would be there. And I thought there'd be a moment when he might make me feel young again, when it would all come back. I even

*imagined, I suppose, that we might kiss. That we
might go out for air, walk too far, remember too
much. I was right about that anyway. We hadn't lingered long around the punch bowl before we'd made
our way outside. Peter had suggested a walk, but
we both knew what was going to happen. And just
before it did, he looked at me, his eyes shining with
not just love, but tears. They filled his long lashes,
making them look like stars.*

"You said you'd wait for me, Annie," he said.

"I have been, Peter. I have."

I put the page back in my diary, where it belonged, and
pressed the book closed.

I woke up early, just before dawn, and went downstairs
to get the paper. It was still dark but the sky was trying to
open up, and the first fingers of orange light hovered above
the houses. A lamp burned softly in Betsy's kitchen next
door. When I stepped outside the dew steamed from the twin
squares of grass flanking the slate walk. Down the block I
could hear the paperboy's bike, the rhythmic *thwack* of each
paper hitting steps. I picked up my damp paper. The first
hints of bacon and coffee drifted by, and I paused a moment
to inhale them. Only when I turned and my cotton gown
swirled against my legs did I see it on the corner of the step:
a bird house. A steep shingled roof, shutters, a chain at the
top where it could be hung. I picked it up and pulled the note
out of its tiny door.

"For Robin Redbreast," it said.

May 20, 2010

Tinsley disappointed me again. It was so unlike her, really. Last year she'd had a lovely backyard party for Ellie's birthday, with homemade cupcakes and a clown and a bean bag toss. This year, she'd decided on an indoor playground called Playmaze, which had the appeal of an Amish corn maze, I suppose—if it had been made entirely of plastic and rubber and rope and stuck in an airport hangar filled with screaming children who had Pepsi stains on their shirts. My first instinct when I walked in was to cover my ears, but I didn't want to fear for my overloaded eyes.

A high school–age girl chirped as she peeled off a nametag for me, clicking her pen: "Hi there, can we have your name for the nametag?"

"Mrs. Harris."

"No first name?"

"My first name is Mrs.," I replied. The nerve!

"A nickname, maybe? Grammy, Gran—"

Her own nametag said KIKI, so I suppose I couldn't fault her; it was part of her DNA.

"No," I said more firmly.

I took the tag from her and affixed it to my felted blazer, and turned to go.

"Oh, ma'am, can I also get your shoes?"

She pointed to a bin full of sneakers.

"Not on your life," I replied as I brushed past her toward the party room that had Ellie's name posted outside. I supposed I'd also be expected to don a party hat and blow a paper horn.

I'd known I was in trouble the minute the invitation arrived—the envelope was neon yellow, which never bodes well. I'd hoped for a simple family celebration, perhaps at another restaurant Ellie liked, with a few little girlfriends who would be invited to spend the night and play flashlight tag. Instead, her entire class was invited to this torture chamber, and from the looks of it, they'd all decided to come. Tom said we'd open presents at home, afterward, but it seemed like cheating to attend that part and not the main part—and since Ellie had addressed the invitation, I came. I brought my camera and would attempt to make myself useful.

There were no children inside the party room, but Tom and Tinsley already looked frazzled, setting up plates and juice boxes on two long tables covered with yellow plastic. They didn't hear me near the door; how could they? You couldn't hear anything in that environment but children screaming, punctuated by an adult calling out a child's absurdly trendy name—Sloan! Madison! Ashley! Would someone please tell me what's wrong with a name like Jane?

Tom's mouth was moving and I couldn't hear the words, but something about the set of Tinsley's jaw made me understand they were arguing.

I stepped in purposefully, closed the door solidly behind me, then cleared my throat.

"Oh hi, Mom," Tom said, startled.

Tinsley's back was to me as she fussed with juice-box positioning. I saw one hand wipe her eye before she turned back around.

"Hi," she said, too brightly.

"Hello," I replied cautiously. "Is there something I can do to help?"

"No, thanks. The pizza will be here in half an hour and the cake's already precut. And the staff here will clean up. That's the beauty of a place like this."

"Yes, that's the beauty," I said, as a body thumped hard against the door outside. I looked through the large window but saw nothing—they bounce, they roll, and they just run off, like deer along the highway.

I pulled juice boxes out of their plastic cages and handed them to Tom. When he finished the tables, Tom and I made small talk while Tinsley picked at her cuticles, something I'd never seen her do before. Then he mentioned his upcoming business trip to New York.

"You know, dear, you should take Tinsley with you. I could watch Ellie overnight."

I felt Tinsley's eyes look up from her hands, cautiously.

"Really? Well, it would be two nights, actually, Mom, are you sure you—"

I tried to hide my joy but I doubt I succeeded; I felt my cheeks light up like Rudolf's nose.

"Of course I could."

"Oh, that's too much for your mother, Tom," Tinsley said, and we both ignored her.

"You could pick her up after school, then, on Thursday and again on Friday?"

"Yes, certainly, no problem. It will be good for you two to get away, don't you think?"

Tinsley said she needed to check on the kids. Her eyes avoided mine as she passed through the door, and her quiet fury was absorbed in the rumble of the corridor outside. The subject was temporarily dropped.

Five pizzas arrived and Tom paid for them, then cut the slices in half again with a cutter he fished out of a canvas bag. Ellie and her classmates showed up a few minutes later, sliding in on socks, their hair staticky and charged. Ellie hugged me and introduced me to two of her friends, Blair and India, before sitting at the head of one of the tables.

"Where's Tinsley?" I asked Tom and he shrugged. It was an empty shrug, not a weighted one. No self-pity, no worry, nothing careless or petty packed inside. I helped him pile pizza on plates as children cried out for pepperoni and plain. "I haven't heard one of you say please," I said, and they all shouted, "Pleeeaaassseee!"

The pizza was decimated and the table covered with twisted, abandoned crusts by the time Tinsley returned, her hair freshly combed. She was wearing a thick coating of pink lip gloss, the kind your hair sticks to in the wind. Some of the pink gloop had landed on her front tooth, but I didn't tell her.

Ellie blew out her candles and I found myself wishing, wishing beyond measure, that Tom and Ellie would be okay. It would have been just as easy to include Tinsley in my wish, but I didn't. As we stood shoulder to shoulder, the three of us cutting cake, plating it, adding forks and doling out napkins,

the smallest of assembly lines, I couldn't help noticing that
Tinsley had also dabbed perfume behind her ears. The scent
of vanilla and musk was odd in the room, competing with
tomato sauce and grape juice.

After the cake was served, the other mothers started to arrive, gently guiding their children out the door, as little sneakers stuck to the floor, squeaking their protest with each step:
we. don't. want. to. go. While I was packing up presents, a man
came in quickly, picking up a girl in his arms, holding her sideways in a way that made her squeal, and made me nervous.
Tom didn't roughhouse with Ellie. Theo hadn't roughhoused
with Tom. I didn't even like the sound of the word, heavy on
the tongue. The man flipped his daughter upright again, and
I felt Tinsley moving toward the two of them, leaning in with
her smile and attention as if they'd performed a trick for an
audience of one. Tinsley didn't touch the man; didn't speak to
him or call his name, but smiled a wide lipsticky smile that he
returned. Their smiles stretched too far, reaching toward each
other like a tightrope they could walk. I squinted: he had dark
hair and he was wearing a sweatshirt, though not a Villanova
one. Was that him? I looked at his hands gripping his daughter.
Were those the fat fingers that had held Tinsley's cheek? Or
was there, god forbid, more than one? I glanced back at Tom
but he was leaning over the cooler, looking for something amid
the ice. Tinsley walked them to the door and said good-bye.
She didn't touch him, but her eyes lingered on him, moving
from face to neck to forearm. I recognized that look.

I slipped out and followed the man and his daughter to
the front desk, where they stopped to get the little girl's shoes.

"Hi, Zach," I said breezily.

"Hello," he replied slowly as he looked up from tying his daughter's shoes, his face trying to place mine.

I smiled as if we were old friends, then watched from the window as he and his daughter skipped out to their Lexus SUV, where a blond woman sat in the passenger seat, bouncing a baby on her lap.

Later, back at the house, Ellie and I carried in her presents while her parents brought in the cooler and the tote bags. Ellie had handed them to me, saying, "Take this one, Grandma, it's a light one," and, "Not that one, it's too heavy." If that had come from Tinsley, I'd find it foolish, but from Ellie it was endearing.

Tinsley went into the kitchen and whistled as she opened cupboards, took down dessert plates, started a pot of coffee. As if she'd been bolstered or fortified by seeing Zach at the party. She and Tom shooed away my offer of help, insisted that I go in the living room with Ellie.

My present looked dull in the pile on the dining room table, with its pale blue paper and the white ribbon I'd curled myself. The others were purple, orange, neon green—and from the looks of the bows, professionally wrapped. I remembered making wrapping paper when Tom was young—white paper that we stamped with happy faces and flower-power stickers. He'd cried when it had been used and thrown away, and Theo told him that was why he was an architect, that it was a terrible job to design something impermanent. That was Theo, always speaking adult to adult. It was as if, after our daughter died, he couldn't stand the thought of anyone being a child.

"Tom," I said brightly, pulling up a chair, "do you remember when we used to design the wrapping paper?"

He turned from the refrigerator, which was old and hummed so loudly I could hear it through the alcove, covering whatever he and Tinsley were or were not saying.

"No, I can't say that I do. I wasn't much of an artist, though."

"Oh, you were fine."

"Not like Dad, though."

I felt the old frisson traveling through me. "Well, it's an unfair comparison."

"No kidding. Ellie, your grandfather's handwriting was nicer than anything I ever drew or painted."

I smiled; Theo did have exquisite handwriting, baroque, almost. You didn't see anything like that anymore.

"I'll show you some more of his letters on Wednesday when you stay over," I said. "You can read them to me this time."

"It's Thursday, Mom," Tom said.

"Oh, oh, uh, yes, of course. Thursday."

Tinsley and Tom exchanged a glance and I wanted to scream. Had she never forgotten a date, an appointment? Had she never shown up for her assignations a half hour late?

"Ann, I just assumed you'd stay here with Ellie," Tinsley said.

"Here?"

"No way! What fun would that be?" Ellie frowned, and I laughed. My feelings precisely!

"We'll give her the emergency cell phone to carry," Tom said to Tinsley. "She'll be fine."

"Oh, of course she will be," Tinsley said and smiled. "Of course."

"Hey, when are we going to open my presents?"

"Hey, right now, kiddo!" Tinsley said. She reached out to ruffle Ellie's hair, but Ellie ducked under her hand.

The first two she unwrapped were dolls that looked like streetwalkers, with short skirts and boots. She sighed and set them aside—Ellie had never been a doll person. She picked up the next one, mine, and shook it mischievously.

"It's not a sports car," I said.

"It's not a playhouse," Ellie replied.

"It's not a puppy," Tom chimed in, and turned to Tinsley.

"What? Oh, um, it's not a spatula!" she said brightly.

"Nice try, Tins," Tom said quietly.

Ellie tore open the paper, then surveyed the white box, which bulged in the middle. She opened the tissue carefully, peeking. Her eyes opened wide. "Is it . . . a cat?"

"No, silly," I laughed.

She pulled out the jacket and gasped. "Grandma!" she cried. A short brown fur jacket, with knit ribbing around the waist and a hood. Exactly what a young girl dreams of. The gentleman at the fur salon that specializes in restyling was certainly right.

"Wow," Tom said.

Ellie was already putting it on. "I had it made a little big, so you could wear it for a while," I explained.

"It's perfect!"

"Wow, it's uh, very grown-up, Ellie," Tinsley said.

"I love it! I'm never taking it off!"

"That's not real fur, is it, Ann?" Tinsley frowned, "Because—"

"Oh no, of course not!" I said. And as I leaned over to zip up the zipper for Ellie, our eyes met and I gave her the universal grandmother-to-grandchild signal.

I winked.

She finished up her presents and I told Tom I'd forgotten something in my car. It was in a dark box on the floor of the backseat; no bow. I carried it in and set it in front of him.

"An early present for you," I said.

"Three months early?" he replied and I shrugged.

The lid of the box came off easily.

"Sneakers?"

"Running shoes," I said firmly. "I hope they fit." I smiled as I gathered the scraps of wrapping paper for the recycling bin.

Tinsley looked up from her nails warily, like someone does when a nurse enters the room with a needle.

September 5, 1967

quick shower

PETER CALLED AT 4:30 AND Emma watched me on the phone intently, as if she knew. Could she hear the difference in my voice? Were there variants every time I opened my mouth, lilting to her brother, stern to her, flat to Theo?

Before we hung up we made plans for Wednesday, at the tavern. He said, "Good-bye, love," and my face flushed; I splashed water on it at the kitchen sink.

I made hamburgers for Emma and me, then kept them warm in the oven while I fed the baby his cereal and applesauce. It was satisfying, his willingness, his swallowing. His gums squeaking against the rubber of the spoon, the flourish of my wrist as we emptied the bowl together.

"Why does he always get to eat first?" Emma whined.

"He eats first because he goes to bed first," I said firmly.

I was pretty certain this was true, that I'd always nestled him in his crib before tucking her in.

After dinner I played a few games of Candy Land with Emma, then made a point of putting the baby down first. He seemed sleepy and didn't fuss when I turned to leave. I watched as his eyes made the progression from open to closed, fluttering the same way Emma's used to, as if he were trying to stay awake and couldn't. I smiled and stood there a few minutes, watching him sleep, synchronizing the rhythm of his rising and falling chest with my own.

I closed the door when I left, but the bell I'd left hanging inside was gone. A wispy fiber of red ribbon trailed between the knob and the wood, like something a forensics lab would unearth.

When I went in to read to Emma, she said she missed Daddy. I cuddled her against my shoulder and asked if there was anything I could do for her instead. She said that maybe a snack would help. We walked down to the kitchen together and I hummed as I made her a grilled cheese sandwich. It smelled buttery, slightly smoky, as I slid it onto the cutting board and cut it into triangles.

But as I watched her eat, all hunger and no hesitation, no gratitude, I felt I was being slowly choked, strangled by bad manners in my own kitchen.

"What do you say?" I asked as she finished.

She looked at me with blank eyes and I realized she had no idea what I wanted her to say. My prompt held no meaning. My aunt Caro told me once that it took over a thousand times of saying something to a dog before it understood the command. How long did it take with children?

I sighed. These were my coworkers—the toddler, the baby. This was my job—the meals, the dishes, the diapers, the tantrums. The world's tiniest, most claustrophobic factory. The hours were unbearable and the conditions were apparently not going to improve.

When Theo came home I told him I had to go pick up milk at the new minimart. How was it possible he didn't hear the lie in my voice? He didn't look up from his floor plans, didn't say anything except, "Fine."

I stood at the door and held my breath, testing him. Let him look up, I thought. Let him notice that something is wrong. He didn't. I left. Milk.

I turned on the car and pulled out of my parking space. After a few blocks I rolled down my window, despite the slight chill, and breathed in the night air gratefully. I kept going in the direction the car was pointing: east. I passed Haverford College and then left our township, driving slowly past the minimart. Its lights struck me as too bright, almost blue compared to the dark edge of the town. Inside a clerk stared out at the street; he looked bored, a look I recognized from a great distance, even without illumination. I changed course slightly and headed southeast, passing through a few towns I hadn't seen in years, and which looked seedier than I remembered, until I crossed the intersection near Route 1. There it was. The shopping mall site that occupied Theo nearly every night and weekend. The construction was nearly complete, and the landscapers had brought in several backhoes to start preparing for the garden beds that dotted the parking lot and hugged the facade. As if they could make up for the large concrete structure by softening it with plants. The sign in front said UPPER VALLEY SHOPPING CEN-TER in curling green type accompanied by an illustration of a tree. What a ridiculous name, I thought. How on earth could something be both "upper" and a "valley"? As I circled around, I saw lights through the window of one entrance, where one of the large "anchor" stores was going in. A group of men rolled white paint along the ceiling, and I commiser-

ated with them. It's terrible to have to work at night, whether
you're diapering a baby or painting a wall, but at least they
had work. At least when they left their house, they had a
destination.

I had to face facts: I had nowhere to go, and I didn't want
to go home.

I headed back to Bryn Mawr and parked at the train
station circle next to a yellow cab and waited for the local to
arrive, as if I had someone to pick up. The cabbie next to me
read a tabloid under the dome light. I wrung my dry hands
and pretended to have a purpose.

When the train pulled up, the conductor got off first,
bouncing a little as he landed. Three other men followed
him, each clutching a briefcase, each wearing a dark coat.
The trio walked past us, toward the larger parking lot at the
town square. The cabbie and I had something in common
now; no one wanted us. He turned out his dome light and
backed out.

After a minute or so I left, too. I didn't set out for Peter's house precisely; the truth was, I knew the address but
not the exact location of the street. He lived in Gladwyne,
where the homes tended to be grander, but the streets leading there were darker and more circuitous, the street signs
small and mossy and barely readable in the dark. It took
me a while to find it. It was barely within the city limits, on
the edge of what most people considered the town. Most of
the driveways wound up hills; Peter's was short, close to the
street. His flat lawn held fits and starts of grass, no trees.
The house was white stucco in parts, dove gray and brown
stone in others. An optimist would call it a cottage. It looked

to have been part of a larger estate, perhaps a caretaker's house. But no one was caretaking now. The stucco was pocked and peeling, and the bluestone walk leading to the front door was cracked and chipped, as thin as fingernails in places. There were no shutters, window boxes, or shrubs; no tendrils of ivy to soften the facade. It was as cold as the shopping center.

A lamp was still lit in the living room. I pulled over and watched the window, not knowing what I expected to see. For twenty minutes nothing moved through the frames of divided light, not a cat or a fly. I don't know if Peter has pets, I thought with a start. I don't know. I saw only a gray sofa and a white lamp. There was nothing on the walls.

I imagined he and his wife were in bed, and left the light on in case one of them needed water, or medicine, or got up to read a book. Surely there was something to read on a low coffee table below my sight line? A trio of magazines, an oversize book of photography? I wanted more for him: books, flowers, art. But even the drapes hid whatever colorful pattern they held, showing only their dull plastic lining.

A cast-iron outdoor light burned at the start of the short walkway, close to the street, illuminating a few forgotten things. The leaves collecting around the light. Petal-less flowers, like undressed mannequins. The silver milkman's box with a dent in its lid. These things made me immeasurably sad. It could have been beautiful here; it must have been once.

I remembered junior year, when Peter was looking at colleges, he'd chosen Yale but had been so tempted by Princeton. He came home from his interview and told me the grounds were so beautiful; the campus was awash in flowers. And when he bought me a corsage for a dance, it was never carnations, but something more unusual: lilies or orchids. How could a man like that live in a house like this?

I didn't know his wife, but people had told me she was pretty. Small and quiet, kind of fragile, Betsy had said. And Peter told me she was an excellent mother, a great cook. I remembered being jealous when he proudly mentioned those things, knowing I hadn't stepped into the world with either of those skills. Mine had been hard earned. When I thought of her—which I didn't often—I'd always imagined her gardening and baking and decorating. And I'd pictured him fixing whatever needed fixing, as comfortable as he was with hammer and nails. But from the looks of their house, I'd been wrong. All wrong.

This was nothing like my own house with its small oases of turquoise bath beads or overflowing window boxes. No. There were no small bright harbingers that someone was trying. It had been lovely once, but now felt worn and broken, and worse than my kitchen had felt forty minutes before.

I left, and went straight home, forgetting the milk.

May 25, 2010

Tom and Tinsley drive Ellie to and from school every day, and from the looks of the Langley car line this afternoon, so does everyone in the school. Whatever happened to buses? When I went to Langley the parking lot was smaller but I couldn't remember it ever being full; no one's parents came unless they were ill. Now the row of minivans and SUVs snaked down the adjacent side street and around the corner; the tedium lasted so long, and was so predictable, people brought newspapers and knitting. I envied them; I had to content myself with filing my fingernails.

Finally I made it to the front of the line and around the horseshoe, and Ellie waved and ran toward the car. I stopped and waited, but she didn't touch the door. I wondered for a moment if my Civic was so outmoded that the door handle style had gone out of fashion; did she not know how to open the door? I motioned to her, get in, get in, aware of the line behind me, but she shook her head. Finally a teacher opened the door and Ellie scrambled in. The woman pulled the seat belt across Ellie's lap as if she was an invalid. I turned back to the front so she wouldn't see my tsk-tsking face. The way these teachers baby these children!

"Was there something wrong with my door?" I asked.

"Oh, only the teachers can touch the cars."

"You can't touch your own car?"

"No. My mom says it has something to do with insurance."

It was our first night and I didn't want anything to ruin it, so I made a conscious effort not to roll my eyes. My plan was as follows: drive Ellie to my house, help her with her homework, play a game or two of Scrabble, then treat her to an early cheeseburger. The following night I thought we'd go out for a movie and popcorn. But I should have known better than to plan—when there's a child involved, you never know how a day might unfold.

When we returned to the house, Ellie dropped her backpack in the foyer and I went to the kitchen and poured goldfish crackers in a bowl. I'd seen them once in Tinsley's cupboard and thought Ellie must like them.

"Bon appétit," I said, brandishing the dish.

She looked at the orange crackers, but hesitated; her hands stayed down at her sides.

"Go on, before I eat them all," I said and smiled.

"It's just that, um, Mom says I need protein after school."

"Well, there's cheese in these," I said.

"That rhymes."

I watched her eat the crackers, holding each by its tail, then biting the heads. A nibbler, like Tom was—the only boy I ever knew who ate nuts one at a time instead of by the fist-ful. We used to sit together in front of a jigsaw puzzle and I'd give him his own bowl of peanuts so I wouldn't be tempted to eat all of them in the time it took him to eat three.

"How much homework do you have?"

"None."

"None?"

"I finished it during free period."

"Would you like to play Scrabble then?"

"Can we play in the attic first?"

I squirmed in my seat, remembering the last time. There was too much up there; it had become a dangerous place to play, like running too close to the highway.

"Please? I want to see Grandpa Theo's pretty handwriting."

"I tell you what, Ellie, I'll bring some things down and we can look through them here."

"Okay," she said quietly. A bit disappointed, but not too. I still had her affection and attention, I thought.

My knee cracked as I went up the stairs. I thought I knew where the rest of the letters were; all bundled together, in the top compartment of one of my family's brown trunks. I opened three trunks before I found them. They were tied with green twine, faded now, next to one of my mother's shoe boxes, which I seemed to recall held more buttons. Remembering Ellie's idea to put them in a pretty bowl on the coffee table, I brought the shoe box down along with the letters.

I spread a few of Theo's letters across the dining room table. His words were always so simple—"I look forward to seeing you next Saturday" or "There's a good play opening in March"—but in his hand they came alive. Only Theo could write the word "like" and have it look like love.

Ellie surveyed her grandfather's swirling handwriting carefully. "Did they teach him this in school?"

"I don't think so. We all learned to write the same way, like you."

"I guess if you look carefully, you can see the regular

handwriting hiding in there," she said, squinting. "He just added some extra dips and swooshes."

"Yes, I see what you mean."

"It must have taken a long time to write them this way."

"No, he was actually quite fast. He always preferred fountain pens, with the liquid ink kind of spreading on its own across the page."

"Liquid ink?"

I got up and showed her one of Theo's old pens from the desk, and she twirled it in her hand like an artifact before setting it down. I'd always thought that because he had to use pencils in his work, he was particular about writing letters with pens. A kind of letting go.

"What's in the other box?"

"Oh, buttons, I believe. Remember what you said about putting them in a jar? I'll get a vase or something."

I stood and went into the kitchen, and left her alone with the box. That's how sure I was of what was in it.

I returned with a stout glass vase to showcase the buttons, but buttons weren't in Ellie's hand. More letters were, tied with velvet ribbon, pink, my mother's favorite color.

My heart sank; my mother had kept my father's letters? Even after what he did to her? I admit, I wasn't that thorough about sorting through papers after she died; it was a frantic time, with the children small and Theo always traveling, and Peter tugging on my sleeve. When I cleaned out her room at the nursing home, she had so little it broke my heart all over again. I just put all her shoe boxes and albums into a trunk; I vaguely recall running a dust cloth over them and lifting the lids just to make sure there were no moths or spiderwebs taking hold, but not reading or organizing anything.

"Who is P. S. Biddle?"

"My mother," I said. "Her maiden name was Phoebe Scott Biddle, but her friends called her P.S. And this"—I untied the bundle and held up the first letter—"must be one of the love letters from my father."

"Oh, let's read it!"

"Go ahead," I said and smiled. At least someone was deriving joy from their relationship.

"'Dear P.S., It is a very cold spring in Boston. The lecture halls are drafty and some of the students attend class with mittens on. I'll be done with exams soon and will meet you in Nantucket on Memorial Day. Tell your father I'm ready to fish. Love, Frank.'"

She looked up and pulled a face, twisted and grotesque, like a squashed pumpkin. "That's not a love letter!"

I couldn't help laughing. A whole new generation disappointed by my father!

"Well, he signed it 'love,'" I countered.

Naturally, my cynicism allowed me to read deeply between his lines—male students didn't wear mittens. My father was staring at a pretty girl wearing angora mittens, while my mother was waiting patiently for him. Why, he'd likely cheated on her the entire length of their relationship, the cad!

"Maybe the rest of them are better," she said.

I shrugged. My father had never been one to gush over anything. Rather like Theo, now that I thought about it, always stammering and at a loss for anything but the plainest words.

"Grandma, some of these have different handwriting."

I took a faded envelope from her hand and squinted at the return address. Jay Stephens. The handwriting was small and even, the envelope bulkier than the ones from my father.

Ellie took out three folded sheets and began to read to herself. Her lips moved ever so slightly, a habit I'd have to work on with her; she was getting too old to do that. Suddenly she started to smile.

"*This* is a love letter!"

"Oh, really," I said, disbelievingly.

She started to read, in that slightly awkward, halting way children do.

"'Darling P.S., do your initials stand for "pretty sweet"? Or "perfectly stellar" or "phenomenally smart," or "particularly suc-cu-lent"?'"

"Let me see that," I said briskly, reaching out to pluck it from her hands.

She yanked it away, laughing, and continued to read. "'In my book, you're all four. Seeing you biking into 'Sconset with that basket of roses—I can't get the image out of my mind. I have half a mind to put a vase of roses on my desk to remind me of you. I've only just left on the ferry and I'm already writing to you, planning our next escape. When I see you, I'm going to—'"

"Hand it over," I said.

"Aw, Grandma, it was just getting good!"

I scanned the rest of the letter. When Jay Stephens saw my mother, he was planning to "'drag you up to the wid-

ows' walk as the sun sets over the jetties and kiss you until
it's time for the green flash on the horizon.'" I read it aloud
to Ellie and she said, "Eww!" Then I explained what jetties
and widows' walks were. I could picture it precisely: the sky
streaked a wild pink, like lipstick applied on a train. The flat
blue water of the harbor. The scent of roses, the sound of bell
buoys. The small square on top of my mother's house felt as
snugly dangerous as the crows' nest on a pirate ship. Ellie was
right: this *was* a love letter.

There were eight envelopes from him in all, spanning the
three months she summered in Nantucket. I went through
the last letter. Jay Stephens didn't say good-bye to her in it; on
the contrary, he made plans to see her the following month,
before she had to close up the house for the season. I reached
for the envelope. The postmark was June 8, 1936, two years
after my parents were married.

The corners of my smile sank; the letter grew heavier in
my hand. Could I be holding my father's side of the story—
that my mother broke his heart first?

"I like the name Jay," Ellie said.

"Do you now?"

"He sounds nice, Grandma. Who was he?"

Good question, I thought. I went back to the date on his
letter, two years after my parents' nuptials. I was born less
than a year later. I reached for Theo's pen and wrote down
"Jay Stephens" and the cities in the postmarks—Greenwich,
New York City, Stowe.

"Grandma, what are you doing?"

"I'm going to call my cousin and see if his mother, my
aunt Caro, ever mentioned this gentleman, if—"

"You mean you never met him? Why don't we just Google him?"

"Excuse me?"

"You know, we'll look him up on the internet."

"He's probably dead by now, Ellie. Mother would have been, what, ninety-six?"

"Courtney's great-grandmother is ninety-three and she smokes cigars."

"But she's not on the internet, dear."

"She could be. People put their family trees on it all the time. Some of the kids in my class got the photos and information for their Generations project that way."

I felt the beginnings of a shudder along my jawline. Dead people's christenings and weddings and vacations sprinkled on the internet in such a fashion? That struck me as worse than having them end up at an auction or in an antiques shop. Whenever I stumbled on something like that in a store, part of me wanted to buy up all the framed daguerreotypes just to keep them out of the public eye. Having them displayed seemed a form of grave robbing.

"Well, maybe another time, sweetheart. We have to clean up for dinner."

She washed her hands and I went upstairs to splash water on my face. I looked in the mirror and saw my mother looking back. I had never resembled my father, something that was a relief to me after he hurt my mother so. I remember how she wept when I went off to college and left her behind in that little bungalow on Aunt Caro's estate. She looked so small, so alone. Do people think of me that way, too, alone in my house?

I dried my face, took a deep breath, and went downstairs. No time to think of such things when I had Ellie to
entertain. Since it was something of a special occasion, I'd decided on the Potting Shed, which was known for its homemade ketchup and pickles. It was an expensive choice, but
since I knew we'd be ordering cheeseburgers, it didn't seem
overly extravagant. And this was my pride and joy after all; I
couldn't justify slumming around with her forever. We left at
six, so I wouldn't have to drive home too late.

"Reservations for Ann Harris," I said and smiled at the
young hostess.

She scanned the book and her smile turned into a frown.

"I'm sorry, we don't have you listed. Could it be under
another name?"

"No, it would be Harris."

"When did you call?"

It was a simple question, honestly asked. But my mind
held no calendar or date book or clock. I blinked and said I
didn't know. The hostess looked back at the half-full restaurant, littered with tables marked RESERVED.

"Would you mind sitting near the bar area?" she asked
and I said no, not at all, and she showed us to a small table
and apologized for the mix-up.

I was pleased to see Ellie put her napkin in her lap before
she looked around the room. It was a lovely space, high ceil-
inged and airy. I remember long ago, the entire structure had
indeed been the potting shed for the Perkins estate, and Mrs.
Perkins had been known to string it with lights and throw
casual dinner parties for fifty people in it, which my parents
were sometimes invited to. When the property was broken

up and rezoned years ago, a family friend vowed to keep the casual dining tradition alive. The room was decorated in a garden motif—watering cans held simple bouquets that sat on sideboards that used to be potting benches. The tables were covered in brown paper with a cache of crayons in a clay pot. The waitresses wore denim work aprons that had pockets for corkscrews and pens. It was all very casual in the most offhand, upscale way imaginable. Ellie seemed quite taken with the condiment tray of five types of pickles, as well as the widemouthed jars that held their famous ketchup. I ordered a glass of house merlot, which they served in a huge snifter.

The burgers were delicious, and the French fries hot and crisp. We finished with mud cake for Ellie, which arrived in a terra-cotta planter. I sipped the last half inch of my wine and had one bite. It was still dusk when we got up to leave; the bar wasn't quite dark yet, and the light looked odd, muddy, like the corner of a closet.

"Annie?" I heard as I opened the door.

"It's a man," Ellie whispered.

I turned around.

"Annie Harris, you son of a gun."

Ellie looked at me, wide eyed and amused.

"Peter," I said softly. I'd seen him several times in the last few years, but from across a room, not up close. From far away, I could only see the difference in his shadow, his extra weight and heft, the reddened tone of his skin. But now I glimpsed the old Peter inside the frame of this new one. His eyes, even half hidden in the flesh of his face, still twinkled. And when he smiled that broad smile his teeth were genuinely white, not the blue-white of people who have them bleached. A man who likes to talk needs nice teeth, I thought, and Peter had always loved to talk, more than any other man I had ever known. I realized with a start that I was smiling, and quickly pulled down the corners of my mouth.

"Aren't you going to introduce me to your granddaughter?"

"I'm Ellie," she said, stepping forward and extending her hand.

"Pleased to meet you. I'm Peter."

"Peter the high school boyfriend who made the bird house?"

"Ellie, who told you that!"

"You did, Grandma," she said and my cheeks went cold. When, exactly, had I told her that? And what else had I let on?

"Yes," he chuckled, "the very same."

"It's a very nice bird house. You should make them for a living."

"I'll consider that vocation in my next life, perhaps."

"What are you doing here, Peter?" I said, swallowing hard.

"Eating dinner," he said, twirling the cherry in his Manhattan. "Like I do most nights before I retire to my bird house making."

"A cherry's not much of a dinner," Ellie pointed out.

"That's why I ordered a steak."

"You eat *here* most nights?"

"Yes, it's less lonely than Wyndon Manor."

I raised my eyebrows, but I may as well have whistled, or said, "Well, la-di-da."

"What's Wyndon Manor?" Ellie asked.

"It's a retirement community, sweetie," he said.

"A *very* nice one," I clarified.

"Sit down. Have a drink with me."

Ellie plopped down next to him.

"Oh, but we have to go," I said.

"No we don't," she replied. "I have no homework."

"Remarkable! I have no homework, either. Come on, Annie, have a drink with your old friend."

I sat down and looked at him as carefully as I could while pretending not to. The lines of his face, the definite jaw and the curve of his cheekbone were still there. Even his neatly trimmed sideburns had the same shape, if not the same color.

He ordered a Shirley Temple for Ellie and a glass of pinot noir for me, and showed Ellie how to play quarters while he told me he'd made a lot of money investing in "dot-coms" with his son-in-law, Michael.

"I haven't spoken to you in years, and the first thing you do is brag about your investments?"

"I was trying to impress you with my success," he chuckled. "Isn't that what you always wanted?" he whispered.

My cheeks flamed. "Don't be silly."

He talked a bit more about people we knew. He asked about Betsy, and if Theo's funeral had been difficult. He mentioned that his wife lived in the health care center of Wyndon Manor and had for nearly ten years. I nodded, not wanting to let on that I already knew this, that Betsy had told me years before.

"And how are your daughters? Are they married?"

"One is, one isn't. Carrie has given me two plump grand-babies in the last five years, and Laura is torturing her boyfriend by traveling all over Europe without him. Every few weeks she emails us pictures of herself with different people she's met, and most of them seem to be gentlemen."

Both of his daughters were frozen in time in my mind: from the faded picture he carried in his wallet. They were four and five then, and looked almost identical, with big smiles like Peter's and the same cowlick in the front.

"Sounds like she's not ready to settle down."

"Oh god, Annie, who is, at that age? Were you? Was I?"

"No." I laughed. "There should be some sort of college you have to go through before they allow you to get married and have children. Something that prepares you."

"But what can prepare you for the surprises life hands you?" he said quietly.

I sighed and fiddled with a dish of peanuts that sat on the bar. "We've both had our share of surprises."

"And drama," he said.

"Tragedy and comedy," I said.

"What are you guys talking about?" Ellie said, turning her eyes to me, then Peter, then back again.

I took a sip of my wine, which was so much better than the other glass I'd had, it was hard not to gulp it down.

"Life," Peter said. "Love."

"Love?" Ellie screwed up her face, and we both laughed.

Peter's left thumb rubbed his wedding ring absently and I remembered this much: he was still married. His wife never fully recovered but he didn't divorce her—not for me, and not for anyone else.

"Things never turn out quite the way you expect, do they?" I said breezily. "In love or in life."

"I thought you'd leave," Peter said quietly.

"What?"

"Who?" Ellie said. "Leave where?"

"Ellie," he said, recovering with a twinkle, "doesn't your grandmother seem like the kind of person who'd live in a big city? I always imagined her walking to a great job at a magazine where she'd write articles or short stories and boss everyone around, then she'd leave to pick up her son from school before walking home to a smart high-rise apartment with a sweeping view of the river."

"Cool," Ellie said.

I burst out laughing, the wine nearly flying. "I'll give you this, Peter: you have always known the right thing to say."

"Have dinner with me next week," he whispered, leaning in. He smelled of whiskey and cherry and salt, a not-unpleasant combination. It reminded me of the Jersey shore, of pink taffy and paper cones full of French fries, cheap but delicious.

"That," I said and smiled, "was *not* the righ—"

"You and Ellie, meet me here."

"I'm free." Ellie's eyes were hopeful; she liked the bar stools, the darkness, the sticky feeling against her hands. She inhaled deeply as she spun in her chair, searching for a whiff of the forbidden.

"I don't think so," I said, but I didn't stop myself from smiling.

We spoke of a few old friends who lived nearby. I told him a bit about Tom's job, where he worked, what he did, but he said he already knew, which struck me as odd. Had he been checking up on us?

Ellie slurped the last bits of soda through her straw, and

I took the sound as a buzzer: it was time to go. The sky was darker when I stood up and told Ellie we had to mosey on.

"Well, if you change your mind about dinner, you know where I am. Every night."

"Yes," I said softly.

He shook Ellie's hand solemnly and leaned over to kiss my cheek. His lips brushed, then lingered a moment. There was no dampness or sound, just a connection. As if he took a tiny part of me with him when he pulled away. I shivered, and made an inane comment about the weather turning chilly.

I walked to the door, his gaze warming the back of my head. What a change, I thought, him watching me go. My head was still spinning when I got out to the parking lot and fumbled for my keys.

I opened the doors and Ellie climbed into the backseat. I turned left out of the lot instead of right, and got turned around on the winding Gladwyne streets. The street markers were the old-fashioned kind, bitter green and small, and I couldn't see them in the darkness. I rubbed my temple; the red wine headache was starting now instead of in the morning.

"I hate driving at night," I fumed. We were trapped in a web of cul-de-sacs; it was ten minutes before we finally stumbled out onto a main artery. Which main artery, I couldn't say.

"Are you okay, Grandma?"

"Yes, yes, don't worry, dear."

"You should get a GPS."

"Nonsense, oh good, there's River Road ahead, we'll cut over."

I was halfway around the curve when the deer came from out of nowhere. Instead of slowing or braking, I swerved to the left, around it, missing it, but sending the car careening across the right lane and back left again, bouncing against the curb. Another car approached and Ellie screamed, "Grandma!" while I finally got the wheel to the right and back straight again. Overcorrection, they call it.

Ellie's sniffling came up from the backseat and I gripped the wheel tighter to stop my hands from shaking. I pulled across the next intersection and parked at the base of someone's driveway.

"We're fine, Ellie," I said, but my heart was racing. "Everything's fine."

"I know," she said softly.

We sat in the strange driveway a few more minutes. When I leaned back to pat Ellie's hand and tell her everything was truly okay, no harm done, I noticed she had her right hand in her pocket. I imagined at first that she was fingering a lucky penny, a marble, some talisman that calmed her.

But then she spoke: "Don't worry, Grandma, I—I won't tell my mother."

"What? Why on earth?"

"She told me to call her if you ever get lost or forget anything."

I breathed as lightly as I could, trying to regulate it, not let too much of anything out.

"Or if you drink more than one glass of wine," she whispered.

"Everyone forgets now and then," I said quietly.

"I forgot Meghan's birthday last year."

"See? We're alike, then."

As I pulled out and inched our way home, I imagined the

small emergency phone nestled in her pocket, waiting to be put into service, waiting for something to go wrong. And I wondered what she would have said to Tinsley about it all— the phrases she would have used, the description of the deer, of the animal who crossed our path when it was too dark out to see.

September 14, 1967

no bath

HOW LONG DID I WAIT for Peter last night? I'm not sure, but I drank three glasses of beer. I only drink beer when I go to "our tavern"—something about the salty-sour scent of the place made me crave it. Beer is what I smell, beer is what I'll have. And beer is the least lonely thing to drink when you're waiting. A bottle of wine is something to be shared. Cocktails are for show—watch me sip daintily, let's make a toast. But beer is acceptably solitary. It lasts a long time. So I drank, and I waited, and he didn't come.

The bartender was beginning to know me; we were at the start of the bar relationship, when you recognize that he knows what you drink, and what you like to eat, and maybe, just maybe what your intentions are. Or the world's intentions for you, I should say. After a half hour or so, he brought out a relish tray, a plastic dish of pickled cucumbers and wavy-edged carrots. A few minutes later, he was more pragmatic. He pulled a bag of chips off the metal clip on the bar and set them on the table.

Finally, he took complete charge. "If your, uh, friend is running late," he sighed, "you may as well order. I can have them make you a small cheeseburger now, and you can order again when he comes."

I nodded, smiled at his wisdom. When the cheeseburger came, I ordered one more beer, knowing it had to be my last. From where I sat, I could see the red phone on the bar. I tried watching it and not watching it. I'd noticed the first night that the bar seemed to have no name—a neon Budweiser sign flashed in the window but only a smudged TAVERN was painted above. If Peter wanted to call, or needed to call, could he? Would he know what to look for in the phone book?

I'd like to say it was a lonely dinner, or that it didn't taste as good without Peter there, that my heart broke and my mascara ran. But that would be a lie. Two men in streaked white aprons did the cooking and the dishes, behind a swinging door. No one cried in the bar. No one had a tantrum. Dionne Warwick and the bartender kept me company. All I had to do was look in his direction and he sauntered over. He asked nothing of me; he was all give. I ate a cheeseburger with mayonnaise and mustard and pickles and had a bag of chips without sharing a single one. Heaven for a mother of two, heaven.

But every half hour or so, I remembered who I was waiting for and wondered where he was. At ten o'clock I considered going back to Peter's house; imagined stumbling upon whatever had kept him. A sick child, out-of-town guests. I pictured it like a diorama, his life, whatever it held, small and torn around the edges, ephemeral as paper.

Finally, close to eleven, in a last burst of he-could-still-walk-in-any-minute hope, I lingered a long time over a silver dish of vanilla ice cream. I saved the thick red cherry for last, waited until it was half frozen and tasted like some other thing entirely, a new category, a food I'd never craved before, a food for which I had no name.

When I picked up the phone and Ellie said, "Something's happened, Grandma," my first words were, "To your mother?"

They flew out of me, light and automatic, and not, I believe, dripping with hope. I would hate myself if they were. Softly she answered that no, it was her father. One of those moments when children realize, suddenly, the chain of relationships. My *daddy* is my grandma's *son.*

Tom had fallen ill with chest pains, and as soon as Bryn Mawr Heart Center heard about how young his father and grandfather had been when they died, they'd ordered a battery of tests. I found this out not from Ellie, on the phone, but from a tearful Tinsley in the hospital corridor.

"He was out jogging with his new shoes." She sniffled.

I bit my tongue, but the thoughts still flew: it's my fault all the way round, then, isn't it, Tinsley? For the shoes, for marrying a man with weak arteries and procreating! I said nothing; one had to be more forgiving of Tinsley at a time like this.

"Well, it's good that he went to the hospital. That he didn't try to, to—"

"Run through it. Tough it out," she said. Our eyes met.

She knew the language of men exercising, of coping with fleeting pain. Of course she did; she ran side by side with one, one younger and stronger whose spent sweatshirts didn't even smell of effort (Ellie had sniffed it). As I observed her trying to rearrange her disarray—hands in her hair, wiping beneath her eyes—a frisson of doubt traveled through me; could I have misread that kiss, that touch, that moment at the birthday party? No. I breathed deeply and surveyed her. She really did look terrible, I must say. Her lovely hair was sticking up on one side where she kept scratching it and fluffing. Her face was swollen from crying, as if she was already at a wake. She blew her nose loudly and when I asked if she had a cold, she looked at me oddly when she said no.

"What did the doctors say?"

"They said they doubted it was serious, they're just being extra cautious."

I nodded; precisely what I'd assumed. Tom was young, after all. Ellie sat a few seats away from us, burrowed into a celebrity magazine that was wrinkled and wet looking from being pawed through. She glanced over at me once or twice and I noticed she was chewing her lip. Poor dear, she was probably scared and confused.

"Why don't I take Ellie down to the cafeteria for lunch?"

"She's already eaten."

"Ice cream then?"

She shook her head. "She had some yesterday."

I sighed. I contented myself with watching Ellie and cataloging what the doctors had done and said. They'd done an EKG earlier, but wanted an ultrasound, an angiogram, and some sort of calcium test for good measure—That's what

Tinsley had said when I arrived. I thought it wouldn't take overly long—it was tests, not surgery—but there did seem to be a lot of people in the waiting room of the heart center.

"When can we see him, do you suppose?"

"They took five vials of blood from his arm," Tinsley replied, and a trail of tears slipped out.

She buried her head in her hands and I had to face facts: Tinsley was not herself. The doctors weren't worried and blood work was not an upsetting procedure.

"Tinsley, darling, have you taken some sort of sedative?"

She shook her head violently.

"I'm not sure I—"

"He has to live, Ann," she sobbed. "He has to."

"Well, he will, dear," I said. "Of course he—" My voice trailed off as I realized this wasn't, after all, about Tom. Not at all. It was about *guilt*.

I cleared my throat and glanced over at Ellie, whose lips were moving silently as she read celebrity trash. I breathed deeply and closed my eyes. Behind my eyelids I saw myself as a young mother, alone, tired, sad, and bored. So bored I could have started a bonfire just to watch something change color. Twitchy, Betsy and I used to call it.

"Tinsley," I said quietly as I rubbed my hand across one eye, "when I was your age I had a love affair."

She looked up slowly. "What?"

"Oh, don't make me say it again." I sighed and patted her hand. "I broke it off eventually, it had to stop, but still."

"*You* had an affair?" Her face took on some color, but her lips curled in distaste.

This was too juvenile to be believed—that she found

an older person's sexual persona upsetting? Did she really think, with her overbite and mop of hair, that she had invented desire?

"Imagine that," I said flatly.

She cleared her throat and blew her nose. "So you made a mistake?"

"No," I said, twisting my face.

"No?"

"No, that's *not* what I'm saying."

"Then what are you saying?"

I could see Peter clearly in that moment. Even in an antiseptic corridor, I could smell the musky cologne that lingered along his jaw. Even sitting on a cold plastic chair that sparked static every time I moved, I could feel the soft pile of his suit coat against my cheek. Even surrounded by stethoscopes and harsh aqua scrubs, I could remember how he always unbuttoned the top button of his oxford-cloth shirt and loosened his tie, as if it was an invitation, a taunt asking me to undo everything else.

"I'm saying it wasn't a mistake. It was the most necessary, and the most beautifully urgent, thing I've ever done, as difficult as it is for you to comprehend my sexual happiness. And I'm saying, I suppose, that I love my son, but that because of my past, I understand almost anything, Tinsley. Almost anything."

"I don't know what you mea—"

"Oh, Tinsley, please," I whispered. "We saw *you*."

She stood up and glanced nervously over at Ellie, who was completely immersed in her magazine. "I don't know what you're suggesting, Ann, but—"

"I'm not suggesting anything, Tinsley, I'm just trying to be . . . human. One woman to another, for god's sake."

She blinked. Her tears were gone now. "I can't believe you'd open up this conversation when your son is in the hospital and your granddaughter is several feet away," she hissed. "Or have you already told my daughter about your affair, like the breast cancer?"

"Now, wait a minute—"

"You," she whispered, "you just want Tom and me to split up so you can have Ellie all to yourself!"

"Tinsley, dear god!"

I reached for her wrist but she yanked away and ran toward the hallway near the nurses' bulletin board. I hurried after her. Ellie was completely oblivious, intent on her reading, swinging her feet from the too-tall chair.

"Tinsley!"

She stopped, then turned slowly to face me.

"Tinsley, this has been a terrible day, so let's—"

"No."

"No?"

"No more, Ann. No more playdates, no more inappropriate conversations, no more manipulating her. It's *over*."

"Tinsley, don't be rash, I—"

"I need some air," she said as she ran toward the exit.

"Do you? Or do you need to call Zach?"

Her face froze for a second, and then she bolted outside, turning left, away from the parking lot and the parade of people streaming in, looking for a way to feel better.

I sat next to Ellie for a long time, fuming, fidgeting. I tore through a *Ladies' Home Journal* that was squashed on the floor. I looked at recipes for spring casseroles and cakes while Ellie stared at starlets in bikinis. She seemed to be scanning the information, as if she'd need it, every inch of it, sometime in the future. Every useless thing, everything her mother wanted her to not see, not know, not worry about. Go, I wanted to cry. Go as far from her and her desires as you need to! I'll be waiting for you with an icebox full of cola and the open mind that skips a generation!

The doctor came out and told us Tom was fine, all his tests were normal, and he thought it was just acid reflux.

"What a relief," I said, and when Ellie and I were ushered into Tom's cubicle, he looked absolutely fine.

"Daddy!" Ellie folded her arms around him. "Are you okay now?"

"Fit as a fiddle," he said and smiled.

"We're so relieved," I said.

"Where's Tins?"

"I, uh, she's not feeling well."

"What?" He screwed up his face.

"I told her to go get something to eat. She's likely in the cafeteria."

He nodded and said she'd been running errands and probably hadn't eaten anything all day. "She shouldn't skip meals," he said, and I nodded.

This was my son, the boy I had raised: a person who noticed things about other people, even when he was having his own medical crisis. This was what Tinsley was missing, was taking for granted: what every woman wanted. To be worried over, just the right amount. I squeezed his hand. My good boy. The image of Zach came to me just then: his swinging his daughter sideways, recklessly, and her attendant squeals of joy. Did Tinsley not want solid and true, but something wilder?

I don't know where Tom's blend of thoughtful and responsible came from. It was impossible to know, ridiculous to care about now; Tom was my son, that was the only thing I knew for sure. When Peter had spread his coat beneath the bleachers of the football field, and we'd lain on it as if we were seventeen and not twenty-nine, he didn't give anything to me that I didn't already have. Tom was mine, all mine, in a way that Emma never was. I had managed to keep him.

We sat and waited for his release papers to come as Ellie chattered on about the things she'd read in the waiting room: did Daddy know, for instance, that bikinis were flattering on most figure types, and that Ellie was definitely old enough to wear one, despite her mother's protests?

Tom laughed and said he'd see, that he'd talk to Mommy on her behalf. What argument, I wondered, would he use? What are you trying to keep her from, Tinsley? The inevitable? Your daughter will get dirty, she will get sick, she will disobey you. She will roll up her skirts and try a cigarette and steal makeup and drink cheap beer because she is human. Like all of us, dear, even you.

June 11, 2010

Tinsley hadn't returned my phone calls to her home phone or her cell phone, so I called Tom's office and left a message with his secretary that I was picking Ellie up at school. I was the first person in the car line, and I waved to Ellie when she pranced down the stairs.

She ran to my car and the teacher didn't think twice about opening my door; I was her grandmother, after all.

"What are you doing here?" Ellie asked as they strapped the seat belt in place.

"We're going for ice cream," I replied.

"On a Tuesday?"

"Why not? School's practically over."

"Mommy said you were sick," she said. "She said I couldn't see you for a while cause you weren't feeling well."

"Oh, I'm all better now, darling."

As we looped around and drove past the rest of the line, I slowed down to a snail's pace as I passed Tinsley's station wagon at the back.

"Wave to your mother," I said cheerily.

Tinsley rolled down her window and shrieked, "Ann!"

"Yes?"

"What are you doing?"

"We're having a playdate!" Ellie yelled from the backseat.

"No!"

"Yes!"

I glanced back and Ellie's face shone with triumph.

"I'll drop her at home in an hour or so," I said and smiled, then, leaning out the window, lowered my voice to just above a whisper. "Along with a photo you might like to see." I pulled away quickly and my tires squealed as if they were delighted, too.

Porter's was the only old-fashioned soda fountain left in all of the Main Line, and it was nestled in a dark corner of downtown Bryn Mawr, tucked between a pharmacy and a dry cleaner. I ordered an egg cream, which I had to explain to Ellie did not contain any actual eggs, and Ellie decided on a banana split.

"I'm going to ruin my dinner," she announced.

"What are you having?"

"Spinach lasagne."

"No great loss," I said, smiling, and she giggled.

When I pulled up to Tinsley's house later that afternoon, she ran outside like a shot and told Ellie to go in and start her homework. Ellie climbed out and thanked me for the ride, wisely not mentioning the ice cream, although I knew Tinsley would find out eventually—Ellie had dripped chocolate sauce on her polo shirt.

"Just so we're clear," Tinsley said after Ellie was safely inside, "if you ever do that again, Ann, I'll—"

"You'll what, Tinsley? Tell Tom? Because I'm sure Tom would love to be told about your boyfriend."

"I don't know what you're talking about."

"I'm talking about this," I said, leaning over and pulling the photo out of the glove compartment.

"This is nothing, I don't, you don't . . . You've been *following* me?"

"No need for that. It's a small world, Tinsley. You ought to be more careful."

"This . . . this proves nothing."

"I wonder if Zach's wife would think so, too."

At the sound of his name, her cheeks went ruddy.

"What do you want?"

"You know what I want."

"Grandparents have no automatic visitation rights in the state of Pennsylvania."

I cocked my head curiously; why would Tinsley know this? Had she asked another lawyer in Tom's firm? And why would she be doing this kind of research?

"Neither do adulterers," I said. "See you next Thursday."

June 12, 2010

Last night I woke at 2 AM, not with a start, suddenly alert, but slowly, as if someone was tapping me gently. I struggled into consciousness, reluctant to release a dream I can't even recall, and I heard the sound then—half knocking, half grinding, a mix of progress and protest.

I sat up. I walked toward the sound, which seemed much less loud now that I was fully awake, and stood in front of the French doors overlooking my backyard, the ones that opened onto a small deck. There was little light from the quarter moon, but I saw the outline of the split railing, the red metal café table and chair. I put my ear to the glass. The rhythm of the sound was familiar, and after a few seconds I smiled in recognition: woodpecker. He missed his bird house, I thought guiltily, and made a mental note to put it back in the morning.

After breakfast I carried the bird house and ladder out to the tree. I stepped beneath the deck to find the Braille of the woodpecker holes, and my breath caught in my chest. I took an enormous step backward, too fast, and I stumbled, my hands crablike behind me, gripping tufts of spring grass. I sat on the soft hill, looking at the hard cantilevered beams Theo had drawn and specified so carefully, which now had a chunk missing on either side, a gnawed V that looked too deep to have been carved by a bird.

Tinsley? Was it possible she'd go this far? She wasn't cut out to be a criminal; adultery was no preparation for it. No. It blinded you to things; it warped your vision. She didn't see what was right in front of her eyes: that there was only one chair on my deck, and only one purpose for it: coffee for an adult in the morning. I suppose Tinsley knew that much: that Ellie would not go out there. But what she should have known, had she been looking carefully, had she been paying attention, had she done her criminal homework, was that I considered that deck a shrine to Theo, and hadn't set foot on it in years.

I got up and called the handyman Betsy had referred me to and asked him to repair the deck. When he came out and saw the damage, he sighed. "Damned squirrels," he said.

"Really?"

"You'd be amazed by what they'll chew through, just for fun."

"You don't think a—person could have done this?"

He blinked at me, considering. "No way. This is squirrel nibbling." Still, he said, any woman living alone needed an alarm system. "If you were my mother, I'd install a camera, too. You could put it somewhere hidden, mount it in a tree or a bird house," he said.

I smiled and looked up at the tree grazing the second-story window and said I'd think about it, indeed I would.

Something to watch over me and worry a little, just the right amount.

June 15, 2010

I decided to go to the Potting Shed alone this time, but I did take something with me in the car: a map. It couldn't be that hard to drive home from Gladwyne in the dark; other people did it all the time. I didn't recall what time it was when Ellie and I had seen Peter there; all I remembered was the darkness and the deer. Still, he'd said he ate dinner there every night, so my thought was to wait in the bar until he showed up. I was looking forward to that fancy red wine and a little adult companionship. Oh, hell, who was I kidding? Companionship? There was still something between us, even after all these years, and it certainly wasn't companionship.

The door to the bar was heavy, fashioned of oak and leaded glass, and it took me a few hearty tugs to wrest it open. I was off balance when I walked in, and thought I must have gone dizzy from exertion. How else to explain why Peter sat two seats away from Tinsley?

I wasn't having a senior moment, and I certainly wasn't mistaken. I may have been wrong about the deck—the next day I saw a rampaging passel of squirrels—but this time things were crystal clear. I recognized Tinsley's singular crop of hair immediately, and had her back not been toward me she would have been close enough to see the shock on

my face. I backed out the door slowly and went to my car
to think. It had to be a coincidence, I told myself. She was
probably meeting a friend there, maybe even Zach. I decided
I had two choices: confront her, or wait until one of them left.
I chose to wait, and I didn't have to wait too long; after a half
hour of cleaning out my glove compartment Tinsley left the
bar alone. No friend—no Zach. I went back in.

"Peter," I said from a few feet away, "is that drink offer
still available?"

"Annie," he said, beaming. He stood up and took both of
my hands in his. "Don't you look radiant tonight."

I pulled my hands back and waved the comment away.
As if I hadn't carefully applied blush so I'd look that way.

"It was pinot noir you had last time, right?"

I nodded and sat down.

"It's funny that you'd take me up on the drink tonight, of
all nights."

"Why?"

"A woman was just in here asking me about you."

I felt blood pooling in my knees; suddenly there was none
left in my head, my neck, anywhere in my body.

"Really?"

"A reporter."

"Was she doing a story on high school reunions?" I
smiled, but the twinkle, I noticed, was gone from his eyes.

"No. She's doing a story on bathtub drownings," he said
quietly, and the whole intent of the evening, the shape and the
form, started to slip away.

I swallowed hard. "And I suppose she said there'd been
another one?"

"Yes. A little boy. And as she was researching the frequency of these types of accidents in the county, she came across the old newspaper article about Emma, the one where I was quoted about ringing the doorbell."

The bartender brought the pinot noir and I took a huge sip, so huge I needed to wipe my chin.

"Peter, I don't think that was a reporter you spoke to."

He looked at me curiously. I was practically shaking, gulping wine.

"Who was it then?"

"My daughter-in-law. She's trying to dig up things to use against me, to try to keep me away from my granddaughter."

"Why would she do that?"

"I found out she was cheating on my son."

He whistled. "That's a fine mess."

"Yes. She knew I'd lost a child, but we've been a bit closed off about the details. She probably suspected something and . . . followed up on her hunch."

"So she's trying to get some leverage, make you seem unfit to grandparent, in case you tell Tom about her affair?"

"Yes."

"Jesus, your own daughter-in-law?"

"Well, you have girls, so you wouldn't know, but daughters-in-law are a different species altogether." I took a deep breath, rubbed my eyes.

He nodded and, finally, for the first time since I'd entered, glanced away, toward a bubble of laughter that emanated from the dining room. His profile in the low light was still handsome; his nose and ears still as small as a boy's, unlike so many older men.

"Tinsley," I sighed, "well, she must have been jumping with joy when she found that article. But how do you suppose she found you so quickly? How did she know you'd be here?"

"She checked every old folks' home in the area, and when she called Wyndon Manor they told her where I eat every night."

"She told you that?"

"No. But I'm a journalist, remember? It's not that difficult."

"Yes, if you can do it, I suppose it isn't," I teased, and he rewarded me with another wide smile.

"Annie," he said, taking my hands into his, "would things have been different? Do you ever wonder?"

"No," I lied.

"Maybe if I had made my money earlier, if I had proved somehow that I was more than a struggling reporter, doing a job anyone could do, after all—"

I set my glass down on the bar carefully before I turned to him, trying to calm myself, my fluttering heart, my suddenly wobbling chin.

"Peter, I was young, I was under a terrible strain."

"I know. And on top of it, your father, what happened to your mother. I don't blame you, Ann, for choosing . . . the security of Theo. I suppose you didn't think I'd amount to anything."

"Oh, Peter," I sighed. "It wasn't that simple."

"Maybe it was. That's why you stayed."

"*I* stayed?" I sputtered, then wiped my lip with my hand. "You stayed, Peter! You were the one glued to the spot!"

"Annie, don't you remember?"

My head swam and I squinted, as if it would help. It was too much, suddenly, this collision of past and present. Weren't we two sets of people, our younger selves and our older ones? I closed my eyes, picturing myself at thirty, the freshness of my face, the reflection of my slim legs in the bathtub water when the afternoon light hit it just so. I tried to hold on to that picture, that person.

"Maybe you've erased it all from your mind," he whispered. "I can't blame you. I don't blame you for anything."

I inhaled briskly, audibly, washing away the moment with a determined smile. I wanted to tell him all was forgiven, and all was forgotten, but it never would be. If we found a way to carry on, it would have to be with a burden on our backs. How could it not be?

"You know what you need?" he said suddenly.

"A cheeseburger?"

"Ouch," he said and smiled. "No, a lawyer."

"What for?"

"A custody and paternity lawyer. You can fight for the right to see Ellie all you like, but given the situation, hadn't you better get an attorney? And hadn't you better be certain she's actually your granddaughter?"

"You don't really think Tinsley's dalliances could have been going on all these years?"

He shrugged. "It's best to be sure, isn't it? And if your daughter-in-law's been unfaithful repeatedly, well, it will at least scare the pants off her."

He looked devilish as he said it, his eyes twinkling like they did when we would think of practical jokes to pull on our friends. He was always planning shenanigans in the boys' locker room after football practice. Innocent things like hiding people's shoes when it snowed. Once his algebra teacher walked into his classroom and found all the chairs gone. He'd carried them all the way down onto the football field, two at a time.

He reached into his wallet, pulled out a card, and handed it to me. A friend of his, he said.

"This is very gracious of you, Peter, under the circumstances."

"Annie, if the circumstances were any different, do you think I'd even know a paternity lawyer?"

"You mean you—"

He waved me away with one hand. "I took one look at his school picture when he was around five, and I knew he wasn't mine."

"This," I sighed, "wasn't exactly the friendly, jovial drink I had in mind."

"Then you'll have to come back another night," he said and smiled.

He tried to cajole me into staying for dinner, but I said no. The last time, we'd taken things a little too fast. It was time, I thought, for us to try it slow again.

September 15, 1967

no breakfast

PETER DIDN'T CALL TO EXPLAIN, he came to the house. He sat in the car and waited until I noticed he was there. The children were napping, so I went out and sat with him, against my better judgment.

I forgave him the minute I opened the car door and saw him, eyes wet, face drawn. I forgave him before I heard his voice, before it cracked, before he pleaded, before his ghastly reason tumbled out. And then, afterward, I felt less forgiving. How to account for this? I was ready for any number of things, for flat tires and out-of-town guests and croup. I could have forgiven a thousand things, but his was worse: his wife had had a seizure. She'd fallen to her knees walking into a neighbor's house to play bridge. Crumpled. Her friends were stunned, thought she was joking with them. Too young to have such a thing happen. He said she was in a coma; he didn't know whether she'd make it through the next day, let alone speak or walk. Her future is up in the air, was what he said. His voice came apart in the telling, actually broke up, like static on the line.

"Oh, Peter, dear god," I said. "What can I do? Do you need help with the children, or with dinner or something?"

He shook his head, explained that his in-laws had come to help.

Sun streamed in the windows, warming the front seat of the old Buick, and I couldn't help thinking that it smelled like Play-Doh and crayons. It smelled like what I was trying to escape.

After a few minutes, he took my hand.

"Don't you see, Ann, that this is a wake-up call?"

"Wake-up call?"

"Life is short," he said through his tears. "I lost you once, and I don't want to be apart from you any longer."

"Peter, you've had a great shock—"

"It shocked me into realizing that I love you and I belong with you. It's always been you, Annie, always."

"Peter, now is not the time to—"

My front door opened. I knew the sound by heart, the creak of wood scraping ever so slightly across slate. I turned my head slowly to the right, dreading what I knew was coming. Emma, on the front porch.

"Go back inside, sweetie," I said, climbing out of the car.

"Who's that man?"

"No one, honey."

"Mommy, I want my bath."

"In a minute."

"No, now! Now, Mommy!"

"I'll wait a bit," Peter whispered. "Go."

When I went upstairs the baby started to cry, so I drew the water and put the children in together. Efficient, I guess you'd call it. And it should have been fun for them, no? Other mothers did this, I knew. There was nothing wrong with trying to get it done fast, even if someone wasn't waiting for me downstairs.

Emma begged for bath bubbles and when I told her it was too slippery for the baby, she whined, splashing her fists repeatedly until I gave in. I tried to direct the capful of Mr. Bubble toward her end of the tub, but of course the baby was delighted. He squealed and splashed his hands; the water was an inch or two higher than he was used to, but he sat up sturdily; I didn't even need to steady him anymore.

I put bubbles on their chins and laughed at their silly faces. It was fun, it was friendly; doesn't it sound like fun? But I was thinking of Peter and his comatose wife and his little house, the defeat of the roof, the old flowers that needed deadheading. So different from the house I grew up in. Our house is old and crumbling, but it's stately. It's always in need of repair, but we always repair it.

I thought of Peter daydreaming of me at the office, the surreptitious phone calls, in contrast to how Theo worked all the time. And I couldn't help thinking of what had started it all, when I found him at my high school reunion and he twirled me around the floor, shocked at my husband being away on business. He said, as he always had, the perfect thing. His words just right even if his house, his life, his marriage were all wrong. "If I was married to you, I would never leave you home alone, Annie, never."

It finally hit me: Peter had no passion, no ambition, for anything but me. He didn't care about his job. He didn't tend his own yard, or scrape the curls of old paint off his house. He always said the right thing, but he didn't always do the right thing.

And that's what I was thinking as I clung to my son, mine, dipping my hand full of water over his hair, smelling his newly washed scalp. He was mine, not Peter's, not Theo's. I'd gone home the night of the reunion, after Peter and I lay beneath the bleachers together and he told me he had always loved me, and that he always would. I'd gone back home after that marvelous release of finally sleeping with Peter, after too much wine and too many cigarettes on the third-base line, I'd gone home and grabbed Theo roughly, wrestling with him almost, in an effort to erase whatever Peter might have done. Two men in the same night, and not so very long afterward, another small man arrived: my son. Mine. He belonged to both of them, or neither of them. I felt the singularity of this, the finality of my life coming together even as Peter's was tearing apart.

I turned around and went to the shelf to get the hooded towel, then shook it out on the floor, and when I turned back, the baby was underwater. Not because he slipped in the bubbles. Not because he wasn't strong enough to sit up for long. No. Because Emma's hands were on his chest, pinning him down.

"Emma!" I screamed. I pulled her off and brought him up, sputtering, startled.

I wrapped him in a towel and held him close as I wagged my finger in her face.

"Don't you ever do that to him again! You could have killed him, Emma, killed him!"

When I stopped talking, I saw it in her eyes: recognition. She knew she could have killed him; she wasn't surprised. Did she know exactly what she was doing?

"I was just playing," she said.

"I'm putting him in the playpen and I want you to think for just a second about what you've done!" I said.

"Okay," she said flatly. That was all, the only word I remember. Dull and ordinary as an old spoon.

I wasn't gone long. A minute? Two? Long enough to diaper the baby and nestle him in his playpen with a pacifier. Long enough to lay him in the light blanket and give him a rattle. That's all. I didn't rock him, or sing to him, or play patty-cake. I hurried back. I did.

But when I returned, there she was, underneath, floating, her hair looking soft, almost delicate. My first thought horrified me: that she'd done it on purpose. She was big and strong, so strong. She was almost four! Did she want me to rescue her as I'd rescued the baby? To save her? And prove that I loved her as much as I loved him?

I pulled her out, dripping, and bent her over my knee, opening her mouth with one hand, thinking she just needed to spit out some water. I hit her with the flat of my hand between the shoulder blades, waiting for the wetness to spill across the floor, but nothing came.

I laid her on the floor and tried desperately to remember the lifesaving course I took the summer before college. I tilted her head, pinched her nose, blew into her mouth.

"Breathe, Emma!" I screamed. "Breathe!"

I ran to the phone and dialed the rescue squad. When they arrived I was still hunched over her, counting breaths. One of them had to pull on my shoulder to move me away. They worked on her for a few minutes and I stood back in the doorway. When they stopped and looked up at me and told me she was gone, all I could think was that the baby had slept through it. How was it possible that Emma wasn't talking and the baby wasn't crying?

The silence. I will always remember the silence.

The police took my statement; no one doubted what I said, or what I did. Of course she was old enough to leave in the bath for a moment. Of course you weren't gone long. Of course, of course. No one doubted. Not Theo, when he came home and held me, broken heart to broken heart. Not the police, not Betsy, not Aunt Caro, no one. And not even Peter, watching from the curb as the ambulance pulled up, watching again as they loaded my daughter's body inside. His soft face was all startled love, no accusation.

"It was me," Peter said to the police. "I rang the doorbell urgently and called her away from the bathroom."

"What time was this, sir?"

"I don't know—but I rang it five or six times," he said. "I should only have rung it twice."

"Must have been important," the patrolman said.

The glance we exchanged held too much; I dropped my gaze. It was more than either of us could bear.

"His wife is terribly ill," I said quietly.

Peter's story provided a worthy distraction; no one needed to know why I'd put the baby in the playpen. No one needed to know what Emma had done. But I know Peter said this for another reason: to take the blame. To make it seem as if it wasn't my fault.

But no—it was only me.

Because only I know how angry I was. How distracted I was. Only I know how I didn't turn back to look at her as I whisked the baby out of the room, not even when I heard the tiniest sound, the small squeak that I know now must have been skin slipping against porcelain. The slippery bubbles popping, falling out of her way. The water just a little too high. The moment before the small wave went in her mouth. The moment before she hit her head.

No. I thought the squeak was the duck. I thought she was squeezing her rubber duck.

June 22, 2010

Tinsley didn't return my phone calls this week about seeing Ellie, so I called Tom at work. I didn't mention that his wife had threatened me and started doing her own private investigative work. No; I didn't "tell on her"; I simply inquired about his health, his new diet, and his work schedule (fine, fine, and not too busy) and mentioned that I'd like to take Ellie swimming at the club. We agreed he'd drop her off on Saturday, and he did.

Ellie bounded up the porch stairs first, bursting in, tossing a navy backpack onto the floor. "Grandma, I have something to show you!"

"You do?"

"Ellie," Tom said slowly, "let me talk to Grandma first."

Her face fell, but I motioned toward the jigsaw puzzle set up in the living room and she took the hint.

"What is it, Tom?"

"Mom, you still see okay, driving and everything?"

"Of course, why?"

"Well, Tinsley seemed to think—"

"Tinsley should mind her own business!"

"Mom, that's not fair. She's just being protective, being helpful, and she, well, she seemed to think you shouldn't be driving anymore. We spoke this morning about it and you have to admit, you're getting more forgetful, and well, maybe it's time to start thinking about—"

"You tell Tinsley," I said, my breath gone ragged as I wagged my finger in his face, "that I see better than she does. You tell her that I see all kinds of things. She'd be *amazed* by what I see. You tell her that. And tell her that what I don't see, the remote-control cameras in my backyard do!"

"Cameras?"

I waved him away. "It's a little security system."

"Okay," he said slowly. "But—you are getting your eyes checked every year, and going to the doctor?"

"Yes," I said firmly. I actually couldn't recall being to the eye doctor in years, but that means nothing. I could have been there last week, I suppose.

"Tom," I said, clearing my throat, "I can't help thinking that all this worrywart nonsense with Tinsley has something to do with what happened to your sister long ago. And since we never really speak of it, I thought perhaps, well, that I should clear the air." I swallowed hard and tried to conjure up as much as I could remember. Would I even be able to answer his most basic questions?

He shrugged. "It's okay, Mom, I know all about it."

"You do?"

"Dad told me everything, a long time ago."

"What did he tell you, dear?"

"He said there was an accident in the tub and that was why you never took a bath anymore. And why you were a little protective of me, growing up."

"Is that . . . all he said?"

"Well, he said if I ever had questions, to just ask. He said it was okay to talk about it with him, but not with you."

"Oh, I'm sorry, Tom. That was probably unfair of him, darling."

"I didn't think so."

"Did you ever . . . wonder about her, though? What your relationship was like when you were little?"

He shrugged. "I was just a baby, Mom."

"Yes," I said softly. "But she was your sister. Your big sister."

He nodded and the silence between us was awkward. There was so much I wanted to say and couldn't.

"Sometimes"—he cleared his throat—"I think I remember her face. I know that's impossible."

"I don't think that's impossible," I said softly.

"It's probably from photos, not from actual memory."

"You used to smile at her when I fed you in the kitchen."

"Really?"

"Yes. I always fed you first, before the rest of us, and that made you happy. It's as if you were flaunting your luck."

"It must have been terrible. For you and Dad, I mean."

"No one ever expects to lose a child," I said. "Not that way." My voice trailed off. I couldn't tell one child how I had turned my back on another. How I had walked away. It didn't matter that everywhere I look I see the same cold pivot: on street corners, in restaurants and shops. Some days it seems so many people are capable of doing exactly what I did. And then there are the other days.

"Well, it's okay, Mom. I never shared many of the details with Tinsley. Just told her the basic facts."

"You didn't? Why?"

"Come on, Mom," he said and smiled, kissing me lightly on the cheek. "She worries so much already."

I swallowed hard. This was the heavy burden of secrets: the longer you held them, the larger they grew, the more people they entangled. I'd never asked him to keep quiet, but because I had, he had.

"Tom, it's not fair for you—"

"It's okay, Mom," he said, his eyes clear and open. "Not everybody needs to know everything."

I supposed he was right; hadn't I lived my life the exact same way? Meting out details here and there, never telling anyone the whole story?

I hugged him good-bye, and as I watched him leave, I felt immensely proud. His wife was a damned adulterous fool but at least he listened to her. At least he protected her. Who wouldn't love a husband like that? His thoughtfulness reminded me of Peter, and I wondered if it had passed from Peter's gentle hands, to mine, to Tom's.

Ellie ran in and grabbed the backpack.

"What did you want to show me?"

"All I can say is, it's too bad you're not in school, Grandma."

"Really? Why is that?"

"Because this would make a great Generations project."

"What would?"

Her eyes widened with excitement. "Jay Stephens!"

She pulled out papers and laid them across the floor. I leaned over and saw that they were printed from a website that had a photo of a tree on it.

"What on earth is this?"

"StephensFamilyTree.com."

I blinked. Surely she had to be kidding—the family had their own website? I'd heard of friends using the internet to fill in some genealogy here and there, but this struck me as dreadfully showy. What kind of people were these?

"Stephens is an awfully common name."

"No, Grandma, he's right here, Jay Stephens of Greenwich. And when you click on him it goes to his history, see? It says he used to be a lawyer, and then started writing articles later on. And here, I found one of the articles he wrote when I searched some magazines. This one is about Nantucket, and how even though he had his heart broken there in 1936, he still loves visiting."

"Dear god," I said.

"Don't worry, he got married to someone else. They had one daughter, named Kingsley. I found her picture."

She pulled the last sheet of paper out of her satchel. Ellie's face was bright as she shared her discovery, but it gave no sign that she recognized what was wildly, sickeningly apparent to me. That this Kingsley person and I looked like we could be sisters. I squinted and looked at it more closely. Her hair was darker, salt and pepper to my salt, but the eyes and lips were the same shape, the cheekbones equally prominent.

I sat down weakly and the chair creaked beneath me.

"Isn't it cool? I found them!"

"Yes, Ellie, it's marvelous," I said quietly.

"And here's the best part, Grandma—Jay Stephens is alive!"

"What?"

"He's ninety-four, and lives in a nursing home in Weston, Connecticut."

She said she'd printed everything out for me and told me I could use my computer to contact them, if I wanted to. I said I'd think about it, not wanting to appear ungrateful. Dear Ellie; she had no idea what she'd done! I told her to gather her things while I tried valiantly to gather my thoughts. I'd always thought I resembled my mother; that was one of the things I imagined drove my father away. But perhaps that wasn't what drove my father away at all. No. How much did he know about the Stephens family? And how often had he tried to tell me?

"Grandma?" Ellie said uncertainly.

"Yes, dear?"

"Do you want me to get you a towel?"

I pressed my palms against my forehead. "I'll get one. I'll just be a minute."

I went into the bathroom and splashed my face with cold water, but it didn't help. The hot tears came and I let them fall, spilling into the sink, mingling with the cold water that was still running.

Finally I shut off the tap. In the mirror my eyes looked red, my skin flushed. It could be mistaken, I hoped, for a happy face. I smiled at myself, testing it out. It would have to do.

I managed to carry on, to get to the club, to find a couple of lounge chairs. There were several other little girls Ellie knew at the snack bar—someone from school, someone from gymnastics—and after she and I had played a few games of catch with a foam ball, she wanted to swim with her friends and I gladly let her. I watched them glide through the water in formation, like dolphins. I pulled a chair closer to the deep end and let the sun wash over me. Let it go, Ann, I told myself. You don't have to do anything with it; just let it go.

When we got home I asked Ellie if she'd go up to the attic with me to find the picture of my mother with the emerald ring. She said she'd try, and mentioned that she was pretty sure it was in a blue album, on the right-hand side of the page.

There were four blue albums; we took two each and combed through them. It was warm in the attic, and the smell of chlorine made it feel small and close.

"Here it is, Grandma," Ellie said, and I leaned in.

A medium shot of my mother and Aunt Caro, their arms looped around each other's neck. My mother looks woozy, almost drunk; her hand rests across her sister's shoulder with the fingers elegant but loose, like a dancer's. The ring is too big; it tilts toward the camera, and catches a small ray of light. That's why Tinsley noticed it, I hoped, the light. In the background, the big Nantucket house was awash in roses, petals overtaking gray shingles.

It was easy to imagine Jay Stephens taking this picture; taking it while my father was working and my mother was summering on the island with her sister. Her sister who knew everything, knew why the ring was inscribed "rose," knew why I'd never seen my mother wear it before.

"Thank you, Ellie," I said quietly.

"Your mother was very beautiful," Ellie said solemnly, as if that explained it, as if all beautiful women knew the whole coded story: what was possible, what could happen, just by breathing your loveliness into the air.

January 24, 1968

eggs and coffee

THE OTHER COUPLES IN THE class are not exactly our type—they're rather flashy and loud, and all seem to be from a neighborhood down by the river—but I don't think that should inhibit our enjoyment. After all, we don't have to socialize with them, just share the dance floor and the dance teacher. But the look on Theo's face when he walks in twenty minutes late and sees the woman in the too-tight orange dress giggling with her partner—he sits next to me wearing his distaste like a coat of arms.

Yes, the studio is a little run down and the teacher looks as if he's been around the block a few times, but we agreed to try, Theo and I. To try to learn to have fun again. To learn to live.

When it's our turn to learn the steps, it's clear we would be better off waltzing or even jitterbugging than learning the Watusi. Theo raises his arms halfheartedly and I swing mine as high as I can, given the scarring on my right side. After a few minutes he tries to mimic the teacher, but he looks like a contortionist. I smile at the ridiculousness of it all, and Theo can't help it, he smiles back.

When the song ends we settle down on our end of the

bench and he puts his arm around me. I'm warm from the dancing, and his arm is too hot, but I leave it there, I let him hold me anyway.

Afterward, at home, mistaking the warmth for tenderness, he asks if it isn't time to start thinking about another baby. I tell him I'm not ready, and he nods.

Theo wants a baby, and I just want a husband.

September 15, 1968

tea and toast
shower

I WAS WAITING UP FOR Theo, that's what I told myself. His flight wasn't due in for hours, but I held out the possibility, the hope, that he'd be back earlier. Surely he wouldn't forget, no matter where he was. The body tells you these things, doesn't it?

My body spent the day with little Tom, but I knew better than to ask too much of it. Not today. I felt loose and small and impermanent. My bones were like a honeycomb. The slightest movement in the wrong direction, a lunge, a reach, or even a gust of wind, could make me crumble. I stayed inside and did as little as possible. I lay on the sofa while Tom stacked blocks in his playpen. I slept when he napped, I ate the jarred toddler apricots he didn't finish. I babied myself until I was capable of less and less, no language, no motor-skilled momentum. The only difference between me and my son was that he smiled and I didn't wear diapers.

Still, this was fine, given the circumstances, was it not? I told myself it was because of the anniversary, and nothing else. It's just this day. I was ready, and ready to tell Theo I was ready, if only he would walk in the door and sit down next to me, and look at me the way he had in college. That's all, Theo. That's all I want.

I fell asleep at eleven with a book across my chest, and hours later my head lifted off the sofa. I heard, distinctly, steps on the porch. I sat up and smoothed my robe, waiting for the jingle of keys, the open door, the cool rush of evening air followed by blue tie, dark suit. They didn't come.

I went to the window and caught a corner of him, like a snapshot taken at the last second. His flannel slacks and blue blazer, the easy gait of an athlete, not a scholar, not a businessman. Not an architect.

The bouquet on my porch was simple: purple pansies in a mason jar. They were packed in, velvety ears overlapping, bits of earth still clinging, against all watery odds, to the bottom of the stems. They were so beautiful and unexpected I stared at them as if I expected something magical— sea horse or mermaid—to swim between the green stalks. Where does a man collect pansies in the middle of the night? Had he torn them from a window box along the way? Had he taken them from his own small garden, overgrown, in need of tilling, the only thing still blooming in his postage-stamp backyard?

The water in the jar was cold. I stood on my porch and held it against my left cheek, the one that had been pressed hotly against the pillow on the sofa. There was no note, and no need for one. Peter remembered, remembered this awful day when I turned my back and lost my daughter. He remembered, and Theo forgot.

It had been months since I'd heard from Peter. After everything that had happened, it was as if there wasn't room for us to maneuver anymore. We didn't discuss it, but we both knew there was no place to go; no place that could contain our weariness. Once, at noon, he'd shown up without calling, and sat in his car until I noticed he was there. When I arrived at the passenger door, he held out a cheeseburger wrapped in wax paper. His tears hit the coated paper and rolled off to one side, onto my hand. I opened my mouth to say something, I don't know what, and he said, Don't, Ann. There's nothing you need to say. And then he drove away.

As I turned to go back inside, Betsy's light went off in her kitchen. Through her window I thought I saw a shape in the darkness, a thick shadow, as if someone was standing in the dark, drinking water, about to go up. Or watching. Watching and worrying. I blinked, and then I didn't see it anymore.

I went to my bedroom and put the pansies on the nightstand. I crawled into bed and reached beneath my pillow for the photo. My fingers scuttled across the cotton, searching for the familiar curled edges, hitting nothing but cold thread. I threw the pillow, pulled the mattress, yanked the bed away from the wall. I saw only baseboard, electrical cord, dust. Beneath the bed sat a lone dark sock.

"No!" I cried beneath my hands, repeating the word as I circled to Theo's side. Suddenly I lifted his pillow, and there she was. Emma on her first birthday in front of her cake. Solemn straight hair, eyes like silty ocean water. Not smiling, but with the possibility of a smile. She was not unhappy, I told myself. She was not.

I took the photo back to my pillow, and fell asleep with the pansies bending over me. They would be long wilted, half dead, before I had the idea again: that it had been a year, and it was time to try for another baby. But the notion proved fleeting, and capable of passing in and out of me like what it was: not a desire, solid and impossible to ignore, but a wish, wispy and as temporary as smoke.

July 10, 2010

I took the photo to Betsy's and snapped it down on her coffee table next to a gaggle of remotes. She asked if it was me, and I said no. She pulled on her reading glasses and surveyed it more closely.

"Well, she could be your sister."

"She could be indeed," I replied, and told her about the love letter and Ellie's internet search.

"I'll be damned," she said softly. Her eyes moved from the photo to my face. She looked at me for a long time, as if memorizing my features. "The resemblance is uncanny."

"I know." I sighed. "It's rather mind blowing."

"So your father may not be your real father?"

"It's beginning to look that way."

"What are you going to do? Are you going to write to her?"

"I already have. Last night."

"I take it you haven't heard back?"

"No. I'm a little worried that she'll burst into her father's room at the nursing home and give him a heart attack."

"Did you think about contacting him first?"

"I did, but he's ancient. It didn't seem fair. I thought I'd start with the daughter. Then maybe take a road trip to Connecticut. Maybe Ellie will come along."

"I could drive."

"I'd like that."

"And . . . you and Ellie really just found all this out?"

"What? Yes, I just told you—"

"So you haven't been keeping this from me, too, for all these years?"

"Whatever do you—"

"Your bird-house boyfriend," she said. "Peter, wasn't it?"

"You knew?"

"I guessed."

My shoulders fell; I slumped a little beneath the missing-world weight. "It was a long time ago."

"I know. And you were ashamed."

I looked over her head, through the window, into our green backyards.

"No I wasn't."

Her laugh rang loud and true, and I joined in. We laughed until tears spilled from our eyes.

"Oh, Ann, when I get back from the chiropractor's we're going to open that bottle of cabernet I've been saving, and we're going to talk about your father and your mother's lovers and this Peter person."

"Or we could just meet him for a drink," I said as she walked me to the door. Her eyes widened as I told her about running into him at the Potting Shed, and she shook her head.

"Well, you've had quite a summer."

"What can I say," I said. "A person can climb only so many trees."

Later that afternoon, I went to the pizzeria and ordered a pie that was half pepperoni, half plain. That was what the man in front of me ordered, the one with the little boy. It sounded right. I sat on a cracked red stool watching them cook it, sliding it with a wooden paddle, wishing I'd picked up Ellie first so she could watch, too.

How many years has it been since I bought a whole pizza pie? Pizzerias were the provenance of young people. The worse a place smelled, the more they liked it. I thought of the soda fountains Ellie and I had visited, the bar and grills, the grease, the beer. Tinsley tried to keep Ellie clean, on the straight and narrow. It was my job, my honor, to get her dirty.

That's why, when I picked her up and she held the pie on her lap, warming it on the way back to my house, the planned activity was filling the window boxes. Two days earlier, we'd chosen the flowers at the garden shop—purple and silver. Purple was Ellie's favorite color. We selected globe thistle, coneflower, and lavender. I threw in some dusty miller for contrast. I sent her home with a small hydrangea plant for Tinsley—a peace offering? A suggestion that she tend to her own garden? Neither. I'd won, after all.

After that business of Tom interrogating me about my "eyesight" and my driving abilities I'd done what I had to do; I'd set Tinsley straight. I went over to her house when Ellie was at day camp and knocked on the door.

She looked agitated, afraid to open it.

"Open up, Tinsley," I sighed. "Or I'll have you arrested for impersonating a reporter."

We sat in the living room and she fidgeted, made small circles with her lower jaw.

"Look," I said, "I didn't follow you that day. We stumbled upon you while we were out. But I'll have you know that I covered for you. I told your daughter that plenty of people kiss each other good-bye and it means nothing. *Nothing*. And that could have been the end of it if you hadn't utterly lost your mind."

"Ann, I—"

I held up my hand. "I have no intention of using that photo. Unless you try to take another child away from me. And then I can't promise what I'll do."

She looked up at the sky and licked her lips. She looked tired suddenly. Older.

"It's over," she said. "With Zach."

"Good," I said. "Then I'm sure you'll have no problem with my seeing Ellie twice a month, minimum, at least until the paternity tests come back."

"Ann!"

"Zach's wife seems nice," I added. "I'd love to get to know her better."

And so it was declared. We had our own constitution now, our little family, built on a solid foundation of lies, secrets, regrets, and debts. But even dark underpinnings can support something solid and light, can they not? Tom mentioned last week that he had taken Tinsley out dancing. Dancing, on a Tuesday night! I could imagine him pulling the dish towel out of her hand, turning off the computer, setting aside the mail, insisting. Doing a little two-step in the kitchen hall, the one I'd taught him, and knew would come in handy some day.

It's impossible to know everything about someone else's life, but I know enough now, and Ellie knows almost as much. I hadn't told her about "blackmailing" Tinsley of course; nor had I mentioned that I was thinking about a trip to Jay Stephens's, or that I'd written to his daughter. I stared at that email a long time before I hit send, making sure every word was just so. "I have something you and your father might like to have back," I'd begun, and then fretted she might think I meant the ring, not the letters. I wasn't ready to give that up. And I think, if Jay's daughter knew the history, my mother's and mine, she'd see that only a few of us deserved to wear that ring. The infidelity ring, I've taken to calling it as I slip it on my finger each morning.

Ellie was wearing dungaree shorts and a tank top, her hair held back by a plaid headband. We ate the pizza and went on the patio to work. I put my rings in a dish on the umbrella table and asked Ellie to remind me to put them on again. I need as much reminding these days as possible.

We did not use gloves. I loved the feel of fresh potting soil on my hands. It was different from any earth I'd touched—lighter, and fluffy, as if it had never been mud or matter, anything other than what it was. That's what I liked about it, I suppose. It held no history, no artifacts. Nothing heavy buried inside.

I showed her how to tap the plants out of the black plastic boxes, how to separate them without tearing them. That was the hardest part. I could tell by the way she watched that she'd never done it before. I didn't embarrass her by asking. Tinsley wasn't a gardener. She called someone to do things, summoned a truck, allowed a small army to descend on her lawn and buzz about until things were finished. Living that way, she saw only ruined and fixed, ugly and beautiful, not the small imperfections, the slow decay. Not the in-between that makes up most of anyone's life.

I thought of Peter's life, as I do occasionally, as the bird house swings above my head. Much of his life has been steady decay. The wife who never got better. The marriage he couldn't leave and couldn't tend. His body, once so slim and elegant, his face that filled out and stretched too far. We all change. My memory, heavy and dark with its burdens, has grown weak in places. I feel it about to snap occasionally, forgetting things. But only unimportant things. Not what matters.

I still live in the same house, with beautiful window boxes that I do myself. I still collect photos in albums, pictures I've taken of Tom and Ellie. My child, my grandchild. The test from the lawyer had proved what I'd known all along. She was Tom's, and Tom was mine. I can picture the connection now, the links of our chromosomes dark and coppery, solid as a chain. But oh, you should have seen the look on the lawyer's face yesterday when I said I might soon need help on another small matter—the DNA of Jay Stephens! His eyebrows rose, his eyes widened. I could hear what he was thinking—that we were the randiest lot imaginable!

"Grandma?" Ellie called. "It looks like we're out of potting soil."

I motioned to the edge of the stone wall. "Just dig up a

little of the dirt over there. It's a little sandy on top, so go a few inches down."

The plants Ellie had tamped down were still loose, so I pressed them harder, squeezing the soil with both hands, circling the plant as if I was making a pie.

"Whoa!" Ellie cried, and I turned.

She held it in the flat of her hand, and I walked over to look, thinking it was a caterpillar or a worm. Instead of soft edges, the warmth of something alive, I saw a cold, rusty edge.

"What is it?"

"I think . . . it's a key!"

We peeled off the dirt together. "It's probably an old house key we kept under the flower pot," I said and smiled.

But as Ellie rinsed it under the hose, I could see I was wrong. The number, 2657, was etched in the top.

"It's either a post-office box key, or a safe-deposit key," I said softly. "From a bank."

"Whose is it?" she cried. "From what bank?"

"It's probably mine," I said, and even though I couldn't remember, I knew damn well it was a lie. A soft lie, I told myself. A gentle one. It didn't count.

"Maybe it's Grandpa Theo's," she said excitedly, and I said maybe, maybe.

"We have to go to all the banks!" she cried. "One by one until we find it."

I breathed out audibly and looked at her, my precious girl. She held the verdigris watering can in one muddy hand. A streak of dirt fell across one cheek. I felt the odd push/pull of being family—that she was mine and yet wholly separate, her own self.

"Maybe next week, Emma," I said softly.

"Ellie," she said.

"What?"

"My name is Ellie, not Emma, Grandma."

I blinked. "Of course it is," I said and smiled. "That's what I said." I spoke breezily, avoiding her eyes, brushing dirt off my pants, off the low wall.

She hesitated a moment after I finished speaking, and I didn't dare look at her. I didn't want to see doubt or judgment in her young eyes.

Finally she spoke. "Could it be . . . my daddy's key, maybe? From when he was a little boy?"

"Anything is possible," I said for perhaps the thousandth time in my life. Most times when people say this, they don't mean it. This time, I did. Hadn't I learned that above all? That everything you believe could be wrong? That there are more chambers to the human heart than you could ever imagine? Who knew how much more we would find if we kept looking, Ellie and I.

"Maybe it's *your* daddy's key," she continued innocently.

I put down my trowel and turned away. My chin puckered like a toddler's. My daddy. How many times had he tried to tell me? How many times had he tried to explain? And Aunt Caro, always walking the tightrope between honoring her sister's secrets, and guiding me toward the truth. Inviting him in, including him. I knew now much of what must have been in my father's letter that day: it had been about my mother and Jay Stephens and my birth. How long it had taken for him to find out. It had likely explained more about the money, the bad investments. The whole picture, not my warped little corner of it. He wasn't without blame, of course. But he was not the thief or adulterer I'd painted him to be. I'd made a critical mistake: I'd continued to look at the adult world through my childhood eyes.

I wiped my tears with my sleeve, feigned a sneeze, then a cough. Gather yourself, Ann.

"Grandma? I'm sorry," Ellie said.

"No, no, it's—"

"I forget sometimes. I forget that your daddy and mommy are dead."

I smiled and reached back to squeeze her dusty hand. Dear girl. Dear, dear girl. Soon she would learn that "dead" is a word that keeps changing its meaning. I know now, more than ever, that nothing is ever really gone. When I walk through my house, or lie alone in my bed, I can still feel the foundation shifting. All of the stories in the attic sway above me, stirring the night air. When I breathe, I take in all of their darkness and light.

Ellie and I stood back and admired our work, how the colors popped against the white of the house, how the charcoal shutters on the first floor looked at home with the silvery accents.

"It's a pretty house," Ellie said, as if reading my mind.

I smiled. It was always that. Theo and I had made sure it was always, always that.

"Ellie," I said suddenly, "marry the fun one."

"What?"

"If you ever have to choose between a man who's serious and a man who's fun, choose the fun one. Promise me."

"Oh . . . kay."

"Now let's put the hose away, shall we?"

She pulled the hose toward her, winding it round an iron frog mounted against the house. It sang slightly as it moved through the wet grass.

"Grandma," she said solemnly, "is my daddy the fun one?"

"Of course he is," I said dramatically. "And you know why he is?" I leaned in close to whisper. "Because he was raised on Coca-Cola and root beer floats!"

We both laughed. She wiped her hands on her dungarees, surveying her muddy knees. She leaned against the new-timber frame beams of the deck above, and picked up one leg to brush the caked bits off.

"I think I need a bath." She giggled.

I looked her up and down. You don't lie to a girl like Ellie. I cleared my throat slowly. "Yes," I said, "indeed you do."

Upstairs I tested the running water in the crook of my elbow before I plugged the drain. I handed her a thick white towel, a fresh bar of soap, and went into my bedroom to wait. She shut the door and I felt the old panic rise in my throat. I willed myself to just sit; just stay put. I heard the water running for a long time, then her contented humming mixed with a splash or two. It sounded like beach, not baptism, but I knew when the door opened again; the room would be different. Her energy, her life force, would be there.

A few seconds of silence went by and I knocked on the door.

"Ellie, are you okay in there?"

"Yes, Grandma," she said. "I'm fine."

Acknowledgments

Special thanks always to the incredibly wise Dorian Karchmar, and to Sarah Walsh, Laura Stern, and especially the smart and decisive Sarah Branham, who stepped in to save the day. To the entire Atria team, from copyediting to sales to promotion to publicity, my eternal gratitude for every little thing you continue to do. Thanks to Adam Shear, Carla Spataro, and Marc Schuster for their early insights, and to my wildly supportive family and friends, especially Sue Redmond, Shirin Danishmend, Carrie Majors, and Joey and TC Scornavacchi. A huge debt is owed to The Liars Club: Gregory Frost, Jonathan Maberry, Dennis Tafoya, Jon McGoran, Marie Lamba, Leslie Banks, Sara Shepard, Merry Jones, Solomon Jones, Ed Pettit, Keith Strunk, and Don Lafferty, all of whom provided advice, cheerleading, and French fries at important junctures.

And a special shout-out to the thousands of book club readers I have met since my first novel debuted. You provided a wealth of encouragement on *The Bird House*. Thanks particularly to Lauren Sullivan, for mentioning the family ring, and to Mary Kay Gaver for helping me to "think like a shrink."

The Bird House

KELLY SIMMONS

A Readers Club Guide

INTRODUCTION

Every family has its secrets. But when you are the last survivor tending to the dark fires of memory, and your own mind is fading, who do you share them with? Your diary or your eight-year-old granddaughter? Or do you simply let them fade away, along with your memory?

The Bird House is a moving story of secrets, lies, and relationships. It is a close look at the hardship and heartbreak that one woman can withstand during a lifetime. As an elderly woman, Ann Biddle is struggling to both remember and come to terms with the life she has led. It is through her young, but wise granddaughter, Ellie, that Ann finds a way to deal with her past and finally reveal the secrets that have come to taint the present.

QUESTIONS AND TOPICS FOR DISCUSSION

1. Ann reveals within the first chapter that her memory is failing. How did this confession affect your reading? Was Ann an unreliable narrator? Explain your answer.

2. Bird houses are a recurring theme throughout the novel—besides the title itself, Ellie chooses bird houses for her "Aspect" school project. Do you think the bird houses hold some sort of symbolism? Why or why not?

3. Throughout the novel, we get bits and pieces of what Ann's husband, Theo, was like. Do you think Ann is fair

with his depiction? If the novel had been narrated by Theo, how do you think he would have described himself? How would his perspective differ from Ann's?

4. In the beginning, Ann describes her daughter-in-law, Tinsley, as almost perfect. She even attributes her granddaughter's wonderful demeanor to Tinsley. When do you see Ann's opinion begin to change? Why do you think it changes so drastically? Do you think they will ever completely resolve their differences?

5. Ann thinks the world of Tom and Ellie. In her mind, they can do no wrong. Do you feel the same? Or do you think she is fiercely loyal to them because they are her flesh and blood?

6. Adultery recurs throughout the novel and is also a shared commonality between Ann, her mother, and Tinsley. How do you think this bonds the women together? Does this shared connection help them relate to one another? Or could it also have an opposite effect on their relationships?

7. Ann, her mother, and Tinsley all have completely different personalities and lead completely different lives. What do you think led each woman to cheat on her partner?

8. There were multiple instances throughout the novel where Ann's daughter, Emma, acts in an odd, and even malicious, manner. Do you think this is a result or an effect of the anger and resentment she feels for losing her daughter at such a young age?

9. Do you blame Ann for her daughter's death? Do you think Ann blames herself? Why do you think she kept this a secret for such a long time?

10. When Ann confronts Tinsley about her affair, she claims to have the best intentions. Do you agree with how Ann handled this discussion? If you were in Ann's position, what would you have done?

11. Ann never gave her father the chance to give his side of the story, and after his death she discovers he was not her biological father. Do you think she should have given him the chance to explain himself? And do you think this was what he was trying to tell her?

12. Ann reveals a great deal about her past, and even present, to Ellie. Do you think this relationship was inappropriate? Why or why not?

13. On page 271, Ann says to Ellie: "'If you ever have to choose between a man who's serious and a man who's fun, choose the fun one. Promise me.'" Do you agree with Ann? Who do you think was the "fun one" and who was the serious one? Theo or Peter?

14. Did you like that the novel was told from only Ann's perspective? Or would you have a more objective, third-person narrator?

ENHANCE YOUR BOOK CLUB

1. Ellie decides to do her school project with the "Aspect" of bird houses. Make your own bird house and share it with the group.

2. Ann and Ellie work very hard to create their family tree for Ellie's school project. Visit www.ancestry.com or pick up a copy of *Shaking the Family Tree: Blue Bloods, Black Sheep, and Other Obsessions of an Accidental Genealogist* by Buzzy Jackson, to learn more about how to make a family tree of your own.

3. Not all elderly people have the family and friends that Ann has. Volunteer at a nursing or retirement home with members from your book club. Sit down with someone and ask her to tell you stories of her past.

4. Learn more about Kelly Simmons on her website at www.ByKellySimmons.com and her blog at www.kellyasimmons.blogspot.com.

A CONVERSATION WITH KELLY SIMMONS

What was your inspiration for *The Bird House*?

My daughter brought home an assignment from school that asked her to do a series of projects based on the family history that required interviewing a grandparent. I thought to myself, hmmmm, this assignment could really backfire, couldn't it? With a troubled grandparent, an innocent little girl, and a few family secrets, all hell could break loose! The idea rattled around in the back of my mind for a year or so while I started two other novels. Then I decided it was too powerful a story to ignore and focused my attention on it.

As your second novel, was the writing process easier or more difficult? What were the differences and similarities in writing *The Bird House* compared to *Standing Still*?

It was a bit easier in the editorial stages because I'd been through the process already. And as with *Standing Still,* I found the voice of the main character quickly. However, the actual writing was more difficult. The structure of *The Bird House,* with its twin diaries forty years apart, entwining and untangling, proved challenging. That being said, the most difficult part for me is always choosing material. I guess because of my advertising background, I'm a brainstormer—I generate lots of ideas for novels.

The main character, Ann, is suffering from early onset of Alzheimer's. Do you personally know anyone suffering from the disease?

Yes, our family has struggled with having a loved one diagnosed, as have several of my friends' families. It's a reality for many people, and in the beginning stages, it's so hard to pinpoint and accept.

How did you research Alzheimer's to make sure Ann's symptoms were realistic?

I interviewed siblings, spouses, and children of Alzheimer's patients, rather than doctors, to hear their stories and to try to get the details right. I wanted the family's perceptions of the symptoms, not the textbook symptoms, if that makes sense.

Why did you decide to write the novel in the first person? Why did you want readers to get only Ann's perspective?

Ann's perspective works best because her faulty memory makes her an unreliable narrator. I wanted readers to feel the tension and the worry of not knowing what she was going to do or say, or if they could trust her version of events. I love ambiguity and subtlety in a story, and so many novels with multiple narrators or an omniscient narrator go overboard and reveal more than is necessary. It's kind of a TMI situation for me. And I guess I am somewhat obsessed with first-person unreliable narrators, as *Standing Still* had one too!

You are a former creative director with a specialization in marketing to women. *The Bird House* is primarily about women, told from a woman's perspective. Do you think you will ever write a novel from a man's perspective? Or would you rather stick to what you know best?

Well, I admit I have a righteous feminist streak, almost as if I was born in another era. I just really feel the indignation and the struggle deeply. Writing male characters can be a joy, but overall, there are so many more women's stories I want to explore.

Your first novel, *Standing Still,* deals with anxiety disorders and abduction, while characters in *The Bird House* cope with Alzheimer's and the death of a child. Why did you choose to pair these dark subject matters in both your novels?

My agent once told me that I was "obsessed with what's hidden." I'm also obsessed with the things I'm afraid of—which are fairly numerous! If you combed through the magazine articles and newspapers I read, the movies I see, the TV I watch—you'd see immediately I have a fascination with gritty stuff—crime and police, mysteries. By melding them into my work, I'm shedding some feminine, suburban, maternal light on them.

Ann and Ellie are very close throughout the novel. Were you close to either of your grandmothers?

I was close to both of them—the book is dedicated to them—and have amazing, warm, hilarious memories of them both. Because my mother was ill when I was young, these relationships were especially important to me.

What are you currently reading? Who are your favorite authors?

I just finished *Little Bee,* which was my choice for my mother-and-daughter book group. A few of my favorite authors are Ann Beattie, John Irving, and Lionel Shriver. But I love so many!

Are you working on a third novel? What is next for Kelly Simmons?

Yes, I'm polishing up a new novel called *The Book Addict.* Words to live by!